It doesn't surprise me to hear that Cassidy Maxwell's landed in London with the job of her dreams, assistant to the U.S. ambassador. Her old friend Eric Barnes would be so proud of her—if only Cassidy hadn't severed ties with him and with everyone else at Saunders immediately after graduation.

Eric's been haunted by his memories of Cassidy for years. After all, his childhood friend was set to become so much more until she vanished from his life without a trace. But it might finally be time to discover the secrets of her past and plunge headlong into the promise of the future. . . .

Dear Reader,

Well, we're getting into the holiday season full tilt, and what better way to begin the celebrations than with some heartwarming reading? Let's get started with Gina Wilkins's *The Borrowed Ring,* next up in her FAMILY FOUND series. A woman trying to track down her family's most mysterious and intriguing foster son finds him and a whole lot more—such as a job posing as his wife! *A Montana Homecoming,* by popular author Allison Leigh, brings home a woman who's spent her life running from her own secrets. But they're about to be revealed, courtesy of her childhood crush, now the local sheriff.

This month, our class reunion series, MOST LIKELY TO…, brings us Jen Safrey's *Secrets of a Good Girl,* in which we learn that the girl most likely to…*do everything* disappeared right after college. Perhaps her secret crush, a former professor, can have some luck tracking her down overseas? We're delighted to have bestselling Blaze author Kristin Hardy visit Special Edition in the first of her HOLIDAY HEARTS books. *Where There's Smoke* introduces us to the first of the devastating Trask brothers. The featured brother this month is a handsome firefighter in Boston. And speaking of delighted—we are absolutely thrilled to welcome RITA® Award nominee and Red Dress Ink and Intimate Moments star Karen Templeton to Special Edition. Although this is her first Special Edition contribution, it feels as if she's coming home. Especially with *Marriage, Interrupted,* in which a pregnant widow meets up once again with the man who got away—her first husband—at her second husband's funeral. We know you're going to enjoy this amazing story as much as we did. And we are so happy to welcome brand-new Golden Heart winner Gail Barrett to Special Edition. *Where He Belongs,* the story of the bad boy who's come back to town to the girl he's never been able to forget, is Gail's first published book.

So enjoy—and remember, next month we continue our celebration….

Gail Chasan
Senior Editor

Please address questions and book requests to:
Silhouette Reader Service
U.S.: 3010 Walden Ave., P.O. Box 1325, Buffalo, NY 14269
Canadian: P.O. Box 609, Fort Erie, Ont. L2A 5X3

Secrets of a Good Girl

JEN SAFREY

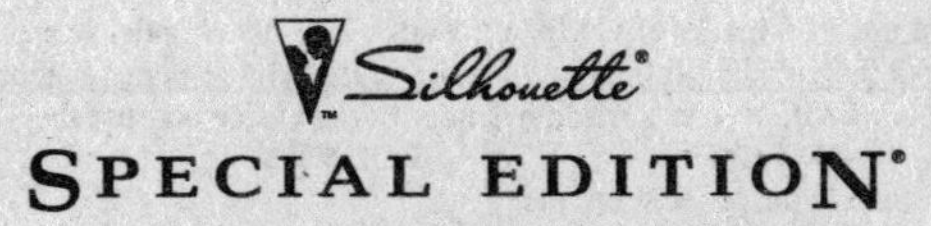

Published by Silhouette Books
America's Publisher of Contemporary Romance

To Crystal Hubbard who, every time I send up a signal, swoops in with her superpowers to save the day.
Thanks, kid.

Special thanks and acknowledgment are given to Jen Safrey for her contribution to the MOST LIKELY TO... series.

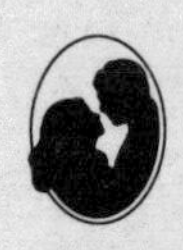

SILHOUETTE BOOKS

ISBN 0-373-24719-2

SECRETS OF A GOOD GIRL

This edition published by arrangement with Harlequin Books S.A.

Visit Silhouette Books at www.eHarlequin.com

Printed in U.S.A.

Books by Jen Safrey

Silhouette Special Edition

A Perfect Pair #1590
Ticket to Love #1697
Secrets of a Good Girl #1719

JEN SAFREY

grew up in Valley Stream, New York, and graduated from Boston University in 1993. She is a nearly ten-year veteran of the news copy desk at the *Boston Herald.* Past and present, she has been a champion baton twirler, an accomplished flutist, an equestrienne, a student of yoga and a belly dancer. Jen would love to hear from readers at jen02106@lycos.com.

Dear Eric,

I wish I could find the strength to face you. I know you'd be so disappointed if you ever learned the truth about me, about what I did. I never meant to hurt you—I care about you more than I ever thought possible.

I can't bring myself to see you. I only wish I had it in me to come clean, to send this letter to you—but it would only make it harder to walk away.

Somehow you must know that you're the only man I could ever love...perhaps someday I'll be able to tell you that.

Yours always,

Cassidy

Prologue

New Jersey, July 1982

It was the kind of hot Saturday that forced suburban families to temporarily abandon cookout plans and take refuge in their air-conditioned bedrooms. On many picnic tables on many lawns, packages of paper plates and bottles of mustard sat unopened on tablecloths unruffled by an absent breeze.

On one lawn, in that thick, still air, Cassidy Maxwell turned cartwheels.

Well, she turned semi-cartwheels. She wasn't very good at them yet.

When Eric Barnes brought a bowl of his mother's potato salad to Cassidy's mother in anticipation of the afternoon cookout, Mrs. Maxwell told him Cassidy had been tumbling in the backyard for two hours, showing some signs of improvement, but no signs of quitting.

Eric, standing on the Maxwells' back porch, relinquished the cold casserole dish and turned to watch Cassidy. Unaware of her audience, she raised her hands up in the air with her fingers spread and palms turned out like an Olympian. She nodded her head once at nobody. Then she threw the weight of her tiny body forward onto her hands. Her waist-length auburn hair swept the ground. She lifted her legs up last, but they were bent strangely and she crumpled at the end of the tumble, collapsing to the ground on her knees. When she jumped up again, Eric could see her knees were two dark grass stains.

Cassidy turned her head, saw her friend Eric and smiled a smile that was always changing as teeth fell out and grew in. She raised her arms again, and now that she had the attention of her favorite person, her fingers and elbows were a little stiffer and her nod was a little prouder. She hurled herself upside-down again, though not as crookedly, and crashed down again, though not as hard.

Eric shook his head, but waited until she wasn't looking to do it. Girls were into weird things. He didn't think falling down all afternoon could be any fun, unless you were maybe playing a good game of touch football or something.

"Want some Kool-Aid, Eric?" Cassidy's mother asked, returning to the screen door. Eric nodded. "What color?"

Eric was grateful for the question. At his house, there was no Kool-Aid because his mother only bought—yuck—real juice. At the Maxwells', a kid not only got Kool-Aid but got a choice of colors. "Purple," he requested.

Mrs. Maxwell disappeared and Cassidy did three more shaky cartwheels before her mother came back to Eric with two glasses. "Give one to Cassidy, will you? I keep telling her to get in here and drink something because it's too hot for that nonsense, but she won't listen. You're the only one she listens to."

Even though it sounded like Mrs. Maxwell was complaining, Eric felt good. "Okay," he said. He took both glasses.

"Cassidy saw another little girl doing cartwheels at the playground this morning when we were on the way to the supermarket," Mrs. Maxwell explained. "Now she's dead set on being able to do them herself, as soon as possible. I don't know whether that kind of ambition is healthy or what."

Eric had a feeling Mrs. Maxwell was talking more to herself than him, mostly because he didn't get what she was talking about, but he kept standing there anyway because it would be rude to leave, and you weren't rude to anyone's mother.

She gazed over his head at her daughter. "Seven years old," she continued, "and already she never does anything halfway. God knows what her father and I are in for when she gets older. Oh, sorry, Eric. I'm just babbling. The heat's frying my brain. Go on."

Eric followed a path of slate-blue stones to the yard. Cassidy picked herself up from where she'd just landed and bounded over to him, smiling, smiling. She hugged him around the waist, squeezing.

"Look out," Eric said, "or I'll spill. Drink this."

She took a glass and drained the whole thing in one swallow. When she smiled again, her lips and few front teeth were the color of violets.

"I'll be back later," Eric said. "I told Sam and Brian I'd play with them before lunch."

Cassidy's face fell.

"I'm coming over for lunch," Eric reminded her. "Me and my mom and dad."

Cassidy nodded, but slowly, and her shoulders began to droop. Eric could feel her disappointment. She didn't need to say it. But then, Cassidy never said much, to him or to anyone. Her mother had said she'd grow out of it. Eric hoped so. He'd rather hear her call him a big poopy-head for going off to play without her than to see her look so sad.

"They're bigger," he tried to explain. "I have to play with my other friends sometimes or else when I get to seventh grade next year, I'll have no one to hang around with. You know what I mean?"

Cassidy just stood there, holding her empty glass.

"You wouldn't like anything we do anyway. What you're doing now is more fun. Keep practicing, and show me when I come back."

Seemingly satisfied, Cassidy placed her glass carefully on the ground, pressing it into the dirt so it wouldn't knock over. Then she ran and leaped into another cartwheel, her worst one yet. She landed on her butt and laughed. Eric laughed, too.

A short time later Eric learned that a bunch of Sam's younger cousins were visiting, and when they began to organize a mega-hide-and-seek, Eric came back for Cassidy. Her mother waved as they hurried two houses up the street, hand in hand.

Eric would never admit it to his friends, but being with Cassidy was fun. Neither had brothers or sisters, and the summer before, when the Maxwells moved in, their parents had gotten together and instructed their kids to play. Mrs. Maxwell had seemed surprised at how well Eric coaxed shy, serious Cassidy out from her shell, and Eric was kind of surprised himself. Now, he often pretended Cassidy was his younger sister, and he reveled in the way she worshipfully tailed him everywhere he went. It was disloyal, but sometimes hanging out with his "real" friends was too much work—the way he had to act like them, wear the same kinds of clothes, make the same kinds of jokes and be careful not to say or to do anything uncool. He was usually successful, but popularity was difficult. Playing with easily impressed Cassidy was less work, and more fun.

Though he'd never admit it to anyone but Cassidy herself. If the guys asked, he was babysitting. Under duress.

The hide-and-seek game was fast and frenetic, despite the worsening heat of the afternoon. Rules were disputed, elbows were scraped, feelings were trampled upon. When mothers began to shout their lunchtime calls, the game was enthusiastically abandoned.

As the last few children scrambled their way from Sam's yard, and Sam's mother began to set their picnic table, Eric turned in a slow circle, searching for Cassidy.

"She's still hiding," he said under his breath. "She's still hiding," he said, louder. "Cassidy! Cassidy!"

"She must have already run home," Sam's mother said, opening hot dog buns.

"No," Eric said, shaking his head. The game hadn't *officially* ended. Cassidy hadn't been found by the "It" person. And Eric knew Cassidy. He knew she'd stay right where she was until she was found. She'd stay until it was Christmas and it snowed on her head.

"Cassidy!" he called again. "Come on out! Game's over! Time for lunch!"

No flash of red-brown hair. No breeze rustling the dandelions in the grass. Nothing.

Big-brother concern filled Eric as he continued the game, alone. He peeked around trees, looked in between the house's corners. "Cassidy! Olly, olly, oxen free! That means come out!"

"She's still hiding?" Sam asked around a mouth of potato chips. "What a dummy."

"Shut up," Eric said. He wandered into the garage, where a car underneath a huge canvas cover was parked among the clutter. Eric kicked and shoved rakes and toolboxes. Then he looked at the car. He peeled back a corner of the cover. "Cassidy?" He pulled it all the way back to reveal a red sports car. In the back of his head, he knew it would be cool and grown-up to admire the car, but he was concentrating on the lump in the back seat.

The car windows were open, and she must have clambered in through one. Now she was balled up in the corner with her little hands covering her face. Eric opened the back door and slid in next to her. She dropped her hands and looked at him.

There was only a sliver of light coming into the garage from a narrow window near the ceiling, but it was enough to glimmer off the wetness spilling from her eyes onto her cheeks.

"You thought I forgot about you?" Eric asked.

Cassidy nodded mutely.

"See, I didn't, did I?"

Cassidy snuffled. She wiped her nose with her bare, dirty forearm.

"If you want to be found, you have to not hide so good. You're the best hider of everyone. I looked all over."

Cassidy allowed a crack of a smile.

Eric wondered, *What would a big brother do?*

He grabbed her and tickled her. Cassidy laughed and kicked. He put an arm around her waist and pulled her from the car. He walked them back to her yard, dangling first her head, then her legs, then her head again. Cassidy squirmed and laughed more.

"There you are," Mrs. Maxwell said. "Cassidy, say hi to Mr. and Mrs. Barnes."

Cassidy, still upside-down under Eric's arm, grinned at his parents and they smiled back. "Eric, be careful," his mother said. "Don't drop her."

"Maybe I will," Eric said, shifting his weight to give Cassidy a dropping feeling. She shrieked with happiness.

"Don't worry," Mrs. Maxwell said to his mother. "She's fallen on her head about fifty-eight times today already."

Eric set Cassidy down, right side up, on the grass. "From now on," he said quietly, so only she could hear, "remember that even if it takes a long time, all you have to do is wait. I'll figure out where you are and I'll always come to get you."

Cassidy tugged on his hands until he brought his face near hers. Then she bumped her forehead onto his, once, twice.

Then she leaped away from him, launched herself into the air and turned a perfect cartwheel, her toes pointing straight up to the sky.

Chapter One

October 2005

One of the strangest things about flying, Eric thought as he sipped his complimentary orange juice and stared out the tiny window, was that the sky seemed just as far away as when you were standing on the ground. Clouds were closer, but the blue sky itself still too far away to touch.

Like Cassidy.

He wasn't used to thinking poetically about anything, really. He'd been like that once. He'd been a young man with his head in the sky, dreaming of his certain romantic future with an auburn-haired woman who'd been destined to be with him as long as he could remember. But when that woman disappeared, that young man then faded away into this older man, an economics expert who thought concretely, who dealt with numbers and facts.

Only a man who'd lost his heart could understand the true concept of risk.

Eric leaned his head back in the uncomfortable coach seat and sighed for the millionth time since takeoff an hour ago. He should have had something stronger than orange juice. Anything to keep him from his own thoughts for the seven hours between Boston and London.

"Are you going to London on business?" he heard a woman ask, and in the split second before he turned his head to the left, he thought, I can't have a casual chat with someone now. I just can't. But the person next to him was a snoozing elderly man.

Eric heard a muffled male response and realized the question came from a woman in the seat behind him. "It's quite a long flight, and I hoped you wouldn't mind talking awhile," she said.

The man said yes in a tone that told Eric the woman was attractive and the man was surprised she'd chosen him to converse with. Eric sighed again. The last thing he felt like doing was listening to a cheery get-to-know-you chat.

On the other hand, he'd already seen the in-flight movie a few months ago, and it hadn't been that great. Maybe eavesdropping would pass the time, help him get away from the musty history museum of his own mind and the full-color portrait of Cassidy Maxwell that was on permanent exhibit there.

"So, are you headed to London on business?" the woman repeated.

Her voice carried over the plane's engines better than the man's did, and when Eric didn't hear his response, he filled in the blank with his own mental answer. *Yes, I am,* he said silently. *I'm going to London on business. Unfinished business.*

"A woman, eh?" Eric heard, and gave a start, wondering if she was a mind reader.

"I'm a psychologist," the woman said to her seatmate. "I can tell when a man's crossing an ocean for a woman. Is she your wife or your girlfriend?"

Neither, Eric answered in his head. He sipped his juice.

"Was she your wife or your girlfriend?"

Neither, Eric repeated silently. Cassidy had never been his girlfriend. She was supposed to be, because they'd planned it that way. For years at Saunders University, they'd whispered their plans. Cassidy's face had shone with anticipation and, every time, he'd felt his own face heating up to match. It was all figured out. Right after her graduation. It was the moment he lived for, drew breath for, waited for…for four long years.

The moment that never came.

"Tell me her name," the psychologist urged. "Just her first name."

"Cassidy," Eric said and, realizing he'd said it out loud, glanced at his neighbor. The man rasped out a snore.

"How long have you known her?"

I met her when she was six and I was eleven.

"And now you're…?"

Thirty-five. But, he said, and the words were hard to say, even just mentally, *I don't know her anymore.*

Cassidy never showed up to her graduation ceremony. Eric never again saw the only girl he'd ever loved. Something had happened. Something to make her run from him and the future they'd planned. Whatever that something was, it was something she never bothered to tell him.

She disappeared ten years ago, he said in his head to the doctor, *but I stopped knowing her before that. I just didn't realize I'd stopped knowing her until she was gone, and then there was nothing I could do.*

The doctor nodded in understanding. At least, in Eric's mind she did. Surprising himself with his candor, he continued his story. *She was like my little sister, tagging around after me all the time. When I went off to college in Massachusetts, to Saunders University, I left all my friends in New Jersey. She was just in junior high, just another friend I was leaving behind. She started writing me these letters. The letters were...see, Cassidy never talked much. We hardly ever even talked on the phone the whole time I knew her. She was quiet. Her face did all her talking.*

The doctor nodded again, scratching on a pad in Eric's imagination.

But these letters— Cassidy was smarter than her age, funny, insightful. I read these letters over and over and saw how she was growing up into someone who... I dated plenty of women in college. But what they had to say could never compare to anything Cassidy wrote me.

The plane shuddered, the kind of shake that would rattle a nervous flyer but caused a veteran traveler like Eric to pick up a napkin in case he spilled his drink.

"Did that scare you?" Eric heard the doctor ask.

Sure, it scared me. She was a kid. I was an adult. Finally, I made an effort to distance myself from her. I answered her letters less frequently. I'm sure she noticed, but when I was a senior, she invited me home anyway for her Sweet Sixteen party.

"I see," the doctor said. She was quite good at her job, Eric thought. She must be expensive. Good thing she wouldn't be charging him.

I was going to blow off the party, stay at school, but her mother called me and asked me to please come, because it would mean so much to Cassidy. I had a feeling Cassidy had told her mother I was giving her the cold shoulder, and I felt very guilty about it because our parents were close, so I said okay. And I went. And...

"Yes?" the doctor asked behind him. Eric closed his eyes.

Cassidy had opened the door for him that evening. The room behind her was colorful and noisy, filled with friends and fun. She was wearing a tight black shirt and fitted black pants. Eric had glanced over her shoulder, searching for her, before he realized he was looking right at her. Her hair shone around her head and shoulders. He'd never seen her wear black before. He'd never seen her wear makeup before, either, not properly. He'd never seen the delicate skin at her collarbone, sprinkled with freckles, and wondered if the skin below it had the same freckles. She'd stared into his eyes then, and he knew that she knew what she'd become, and what she could do to him.

And later, a few hours later, she'd pulled him into the hall, away from her high school friends, and leaned in, and…

I'm sorry, Doctor, Eric said silently, opening his eyes. *There are exactly three moments in my past that I never allow myself to remember. I remember they happened, but I can't put myself back there again because I can't live with that intense pain. This is the first of those three moments.*

"It's all right," the doctor said.

Eric had fled that night, before the party had even ended. Fled straight to the train station, headed back to Saunders, and tried for the rest of that year to forget Cassidy Maxwell.

"Could you?" the doctor asked.

No, I couldn't.

The next year, Cassidy arrived with her suitcases at Saunders, having just graduated as valedictorian, and signed up as a political science major. Just like Eric. He was now a Saunders grad, but he had an impossible time tearing himself away from the campus now that it had suddenly become more beautiful. He was making political contacts and headway, but found himself visiting Saunders often, dropping in on Professor Gilbert Harrison many times to talk. He didn't recall what he'd said to tip the professor off, but one day Gilbert tipped him off about an assistant teaching position in the poli-sci department, and a couple of days later, Eric was standing in front of a lecture hall with Cassidy in the front row.

"That must have been hard," the doctor said with sympathy.

It was hard, all right. *He* had been hard, watching Cassidy every day. Cassidy, who'd never verbally strung two sentences together in all the years Eric had known her, would raise her hand and wax brilliantly about any political topic, would debate any controversy with moxie. Young men and women alike were taken with her, and wanted to study with her, have dinner with her, be her friend or more.

But Cassidy's biggest smiles were reserved for the person she'd been giving them to since she was a child. Eric could read those smiles as well as he always could. She wanted him. She knew he wanted her.

"Then what?" the doctor asked.

Cassidy respected the distance her old friend put between them. Even when that semester ended, he was still a faculty member, and both understood—without speaking to each other about it—that the teacher-student relationship had to be kept that way. But Eric had to be near her, had to be with her. They met off campus many times, and during those times, Cassidy reverted to her wordless ways. They brushed hands in a jazz club. He breathed in the scent of her neck as he pulled out her chair at a coffeehouse. Finally he found himself at four in the morning, sitting with Cassidy under the huge oak on the quad, the entire campus asleep around them.

I'm sorry, Doctor, Eric said in his mind. *What I said, what she said, the promise we made—this is the second moment I can't let myself remember.*

"No problem," the doctor said.

What Cassidy and Eric had vowed to each other kept him wide-eyed awake, excitedly alive, until Cassidy's last semester as a senior. Then something… A toothache had sent Cassidy into emergency oral surgery, and she was laid up. Eric had tried to help her keep up with her work, but stubborn Cassidy had pushed him away, wanted to do everything herself. He'd seen less and less of her, and when he had seen her, she was pale, thinner, with bags under her eyes as big as coin purses. That last time he'd seen her, two days before her graduation, she'd been in the library, scribbling madly into a notebook. When he'd tapped her on the shoulder, she'd jumped, stared at him with frightening, bloodshot eyes, and bolted from the library, mumbling an apology, or something that sounded like it.

Graduation day dawned. A horde of black-robed seniors hurtled themselves off the main building's stone stairs, shrieking with joy. Eric waited in the spot they'd chosen. Waited with a locket in his sweating hand, the one he'd wanted to give Cassidy as they began their new future together. The quad emptied around him as he stood alone in that moment…

"I understand," the doctor said.

Eric was glad. That third moment he couldn't let himself remember, that one was the hardest. The one he'd had no explanation for—for ten years.

He clutched the empty plastic cup in his hand, crumpling it, and suddenly a smiling flight attendant was there. He dropped it in the trash bag she held out and leaned back again.

He never searched Cassidy out. He'd refused to. His pride wouldn't let him. But now, Professor Gilbert needed help from his former students to save his job, and everyone knew reliable Cassidy Maxwell would do anything for a friend. One conversation with a fellow Saunders alum and suddenly Eric was over the Atlantic Ocean, traveling to another continent to bring the only woman in his heart back into his life.

The main lights in the cabin blinked out. People around Eric reached for headsets and neck pillows, reclining their seats back.

"I'll let you get some sleep. Good luck on your trip," the doctor said.

Eric knew the luck wasn't for him, but decided to take a little anyway. He was about to need it.

All he'd ever wanted to do was to help people. That's why he became a professor. He wanted to teach young people, guide them, assist them in any way he could in making decisions that could affect the rest of their lives.

Now, there was one person Gilbert Harrison was powerless to help. Himself.

Gilbert laid his head down on his cluttered desk. His forehead knocked several file folders to the floor and he heard papers scatter, but he didn't bother to bend down to pick them up. He just closed his eyes and listened to silence. It was nearly midnight, but he couldn't go home. These days, it was hard to leave his office, because each time he did, he was forced to wonder if it would be the last time.

He'd done so much in this office, for so many students, for so many years.

The Board of Directors' investigation, led by the vindictive Alex Broadstreet, was a humiliating chapter in Gilbert's professional life at Saunders University. So far, he'd had his name dragged through the mud and he'd been forced to ask former students to return to campus to appeal to the board on his behalf. It was ironic, considering they didn't even know the half of what he'd done for each of them, but he had taken a chance that their successes as alumni could sway the board and save his job. The only job he ever wanted to do.

And just as a candle of hope had begun to flicker, it was blown out again when he got Eric Barnes's phone call today. Eric had called from Logan International Airport, about to board a plane to London to bring Cassidy Maxwell back to Massachusetts.

"Are you sure you want to do that?" Gilbert had asked after a stunned pause.

"Ella Gardner and I had lunch last week," Eric had answered. "She told me about you, and your trouble there at Saunders. Are you all right?"

"I'm hanging in there," Gilbert had answered honestly.

"Look, you know you're everyone's favorite professor. It's our turn to help you. I've thought this over. I *know*—Cassidy—would want to help you if she could. And I'm going to London to ask her."

He can barely say her name, Gilbert had thought. Eric was as afraid to face Cassidy Maxwell as Gilbert was, though for entirely different reasons. "I don't think that's necessary," Gilbert said, measuring his words. "She's now Ambassador Alan Cole's chief go-to girl."

Good for her, he thought silently, in spite of his growing fear. "She has a busy schedule. Don't bother her with this, with my problems."

"You know her, Professor. If she finds out about this later, she'll be angry no one told her."

"True," Gilbert had been forced to admit. "Why not just give her a call or e-mail her?"

"I think she'll be more likely to come back if she's summoned in person. Besides..." His voice had trailed off and Gilbert had waited a moment before Eric added, "Phone calls and e-mails are too easy to ignore. And she's done an admirable job of ignoring me for the past ten years. For your sake, I need to talk to her in person."

"For my sake, huh?"

Gilbert could tell by the silence that perhaps a decade wasn't long enough to heal a broken heart. "Are you sure you are ready for this?"

"It's time," Eric had said shakily, then more forcefully, repeated, "It's time."

"What if she doesn't..."

"I don't plan on dragging her back by her hair. I'll tell her what's going on and leave it up to her."

Gilbert had sighed then. Eric knew what dire straits

his old professor was in. If Gilbert protested any more, Eric would grow suspicious, and he couldn't afford that. He'd wished his former student luck and hung up.

Then he'd sat here in his office chair, without moving, for hours. His anxiety, already high from his job crisis, had expanded until he felt he'd be eaten from the inside out.

He lifted his head and looked out the tiny window next to his desk, but saw nothing but his own reflection. That was the last thing he wanted to see: Gilbert Harrison staring into himself. He snapped off the small desk lamp and sat in darkness. He could see the outline of leaves against the sky. When a breeze blew through, the leaves fluttered slackly, beginning to lose their hold on the branches. In harsh New England winter afternoons, Gilbert could see the Liberal Arts building across the street. In late spring, the lush greenery again obstructed his view. He had noticed this every year—for thirty years.

In the last few weeks, he'd seen his past come back to him: Saunders sweethearts David and Sandra Westport, crack attorney Nate Williams, the still-beautiful Kathryn Price, sharp-as-a-tack Jane Jackson, a transformed Dr. Jacob Weber. He'd been glad to see each of them. His heart had puffed with pride as he'd examined their older, different faces and heard their stories.

But Cassidy Maxwell might come back, as well.

Her former classmates had gotten wind of her possible return and were excited at the prospect of seeing her again. She had been the good girl on campus, a brilliant scholar, a willing tutor, everyone's friend. The alumni were convinced she could play a major role in keeping Gilbert on the Saunders faculty.

"Won't it be great to see her again?" they asked Gilbert, one by one. "It's been so long! Isn't it terrific she might come back?"

What no one would have ever guessed was that if Gilbert had his way, he'd keep good-girl Cassidy as far away from Saunders University as possible. The other side of an ocean wasn't even far enough.

If Cassidy came back, she'd also bring back Gilbert's deepest, darkest secret. A secret she'd discovered a long time ago, accidentally. A secret no one else knew.

That secret could not only destroy Gilbert's career, but his entire life as he knew it—his and the lives of others.

Gilbert put his head in his hands again. *I'm so sorry, Eric,* he thought with shame. *I've never before wanted one of my students to fail.*

But I hope you do.

Chapter Two

"What do you mean, we can't get the Château Clinet?" Cassidy asked.

She held the phone slightly away from her ear as the wine supplier offered a rambling explanation for not being able to meet Cassidy's wine order for the ambassador's reception tonight. Unfortunately, Cassidy didn't have much time for explanations. She was more a solutions person.

"Right," Cassidy interrupted. "Well, since it won't do to be without wine tonight, we need a Plan B. Can you replace the Château Clinet with Château Clos Fourtet? If I can't get the Pomerol, the Saint-Emilion should be just as good." The wine supplier put her on hold to check and, lifting her chin to her open office door, Cassidy called, "Sophie?"

The eager junior staffer appeared almost immediately. Cassidy waved her in and handed her a stack of paper samples. "If you'd please call the paper shop, the number's on top, tell them the stock they recommended for the official stationery is excellent, but the color was a little dark. Tell them the light cream is what we want."

"Right away." As Sophie scurried out, the wine supplier came back to the phone to report they could indeed deliver the needed quantity of Château Clos Fourtet to the ambassador's residence that afternoon. Cassidy was relieved. Ambassador Alan Cole was hosting a Winfield House reception that night for his good friend, the artistic director for a prominent Chicago ballet company, who was in London to collaborate on a project with the Royal Ballet. The ambassador was pleased to have his friend in town, and Cassidy didn't want any problems, no matter how minor.

Of course, as Ambassador Cole's office management specialist, Cassidy's job was to ensure *all* U.S. Embassy problems were kept to a very bare minimum.

Cassidy thanked the wine supplier and hung up, and the moment she lifted her finger from the End button, her cell phone jingled again. "Maxwell," she answered. She looked at her index finger, where a permanent dent seemed to have formed. The front desk secretary informed her that the plumber had arrived.

"I'm on my way," Cassidy said. She breezed through the front office, where many people were typing, faxing, taking calls. Charles, another junior staffer, stood and sprinted over to her. People in the embassy were always running to catch up to Cassidy.

"MP Violet Ashton wants to meet with the ambassador as soon as possible," he said. Cassidy was appreciative that Charles knew to waste no time on pleasantries. "And Sir Neville Pritchard of the House of Lords wants to see the ambassador, also."

"Can I assume MP Ashton wants to meet regarding the ambassador's Northern Ireland peace initiative?"

"Correct."

"Right, tell her tomorrow is fine. Anytime. I'll fit the agenda around her. And Sir Pritchard, tell him Wednesday or Thursday of next week, midafternoon is best."

"All right."

Cassidy left the large room, rounded several corners, walked down several long hallways. The sharp heels of her black leather ankle boots clicked authoritatively, a sound she secretly liked.

She greeted the plumber at the main entrance and escorted him up three floors. Standing together in the otherwise empty elevator, he gave her a friendly, appraising glance. She winced as the elevator dinged and wordlessly led him to a small room on the left.

Cassidy maneuvered many locks with keys and codes and eventually let them both into a small nondescript room. She perched on a table and waited as the plumber investigated the leak Cassidy had reported last week. She would have to wait until he was done, as only a small handful of people had the top-secret clearance to even enter this room, which was filled with classified files.

She glanced at her watch. She wanted to call the public affairs department before two o'clock, and there was that meeting at three…

Cassidy crossed her legs at the knee and noticed splotchy raindrop marks on her shoes. She pulled a tissue out of her pocket and swiped at them. At dawn, she'd been out on a Heathrow Airport tarmac with bodyguards to greet an assistant U.S. secretary of state, and although she'd been standing under an umbrella, London's legendary dreary rain had soaked her feet and dampened the cuffs of her trousers. She'd had to grin and bear the splooshing between her toes as she'd escorted the official in a limo to his breakfast meeting with the ambassador.

At least the sun was out again, but Cassidy was annoyed to be even thinking about the weather. She was so accustomed to constant motion and decision-making that it was maddening to have more than five minutes of downtime.

Downtime led to quiet contemplation, to thinking. Cassidy had trained herself long ago not to sit and think. Keep moving, she told herself, from the minute she woke up every morning to the last moment before she dropped her head on the pillow. Keep moving.

Don't stop.

She whipped out a small pad of paper and pen from an inside pocket of her fitted black pin-striped jacket and began to scribble a list of things to do in the next hour. Call Winfield House and ask the head housekeeper to fax her tonight's menu to make sure nothing was forgotten, update the ambassador's schedule for tomorrow to fit in the meeting with the MP—Cassidy's stomach rumbled. Oh, yes, get lunch. If time permits.

After the plumber indicated he was finished but would need to get into a rest room one floor above, Cassidy let them both out, secured the room and called Charles to take the worker to the rest room. Then she returned to the front office and resumed running around for several more hours.

At promptly three, Cassidy escorted five men and one woman to a public meeting room. They were representatives from an American lingerie company called Underneath It All. They wanted to open a London branch, and they were set to make a pitch for support from the ambassador.

But Ambassador Cole had not yet returned from his appointments. Cassidy sighed, and as she chatted informally with the businesspeople, her cell phone rang. "Maxwell."

"Cassidy, it's me," Ambassador Cole said, but his voice sounded very far away, and strained through static.

"I can't hear you well, Ambassador."

"Bad connection. Listen, I'm running late. We're sitting here in traffic the likes of which I've never seen."

"Since yesterday?" Cassidy couldn't help herself.

"I did say that yesterday, didn't I?" The ambassador chuckled. "Cassidy, you'll hold down the fort." It wasn't a question. It was a confident statement.

"Yes."

"I shouldn't be longer than a half hour. Shouldn't, but

who knows for sure. There's a double-decker bus in front of the car, and we can't see a bloody thing."

Cassidy smiled. Like herself, Ambassador Cole hadn't picked up a British accent, but had managed to adopt several choice phrases. "Don't worry. We're good to go here. We'll get things done."

"I know you will."

"I'm fitting MP Ashton in tomorrow." She decided not to tell him about the averted wine crisis. It would just sound like showing off. "And there are a few documents on your desk that need approval before I send them out."

"Thank you, Cassidy."

He clicked off and Cassidy faced the small group. "That was the ambassador. He's running a bit behind. If you spend more than two days in London, you'll know that isn't an unusual scenario."

The guests chuckled.

"Right," Cassidy said. "I'll arrange for tea service, and while we wait for the ambassador, you can ask me anything you like about London. I've been working here at the embassy for just about ten years, so I should be able to answer just about any question you might have while we wait."

One phone call and ten minutes later, Cassidy's fellow Americans were pouring tea and looking delighted about it. Cassidy remembered when she first arrived in London and how she thought tea was so refined and classy and relaxed. Now she was lucky to gulp down two sips from a takeaway thermos on the way to a meeting.

The businesspeople asked Cassidy many questions about many topics, from London's shopping areas to the weather to the hot-button political issues. They seemed pleased with Cassidy's straightforward, knowledgeable answers, and the more information she supplied, the more questions they asked.

Cassidy loved her job, but often felt tired at the end of the day, and not from running around. She often grew weary from all her talking. She'd never talked much, as a child, as a teenager. She'd chosen not to. She supposed she'd always liked to watch life, and listen.

At the embassy, she had to be an effective communicator, and she believed she was, but sometimes she secretly longed for the time when she could say nothing and have her feelings be understood anyway. The person who never failed at that understanding was—

Not in her life now.

Cassidy shook her head with a tiny motion and kept talking so she didn't have to think about him, about anything. When it came to suppressing unthinkable thoughts, she was a professional with a decade of experience.

"Ms. Maxwell," said one of the men. She looked at him. He was easily the youngest one in the room, perhaps the most eager to show his bosses that he meant business. He reached into a large portfolio at his feet and pulled out a posterboard featuring a black-and-white photo of a scantily clad couple in a heated embrace. "You've been so helpful, that I think we can use your personal opinion. Tell us, how do you think Brits would feel about this poster on a Piccadilly Circus billboard?"

Cassidy looked at the poster, but a flash of movement caught her gaze and coaxed it over the man's shoulder. She could see through the glass wall of the meeting room, straight to the embassy lobby.

Straight into a pair of eyes.

Cassidy sucked in a breath so hard she almost choked.

Bottomless black eyes.

From here, a stranger might think the distance made those eyes look black. But Cassidy was no stranger, and she knew if she walked out of the meeting room, walked closer and closer until she was an inch away, they would still be an almost-impossible ink-black.

Those eyes—Cassidy remembered how as a smitten child, as a teenager with a crush, as a young woman in love, she would do anything to make those eyes look her way. Then, after her mistakes, she feared she could never look into those eyes again. So she'd run away.

There was nowhere to run now.

Every memory she'd banished to the far corners of her mind now leaped out like monsters in a haunted house. Every single thought she'd outrun now clawed at her back.

The only man she ever loved was standing right in front of her again, and there was no escape.

Eric didn't smile. He didn't wave or nod. He just held her gaze, and Cassidy was forced to face the hurt she'd inflicted.

"Ms. Maxwell?" she heard, and snapped her attention back to the poster. "Ms. Maxwell? How do you think people in London will feel about this ad?"

Cassidy parted her lips, intending to give a professional response, but her mind tricked her into honesty. "Stunned," she mumbled. She looked over the man's shoulder. Eric hadn't moved. "Shocked," she whispered.

The uncomfortable rustling in the room brought her back once again. "Excuse me?" the one woman asked. "I rather thought Europeans were less reserved than Americans."

"We intended a sexy, suggestive effect, not something offensive," another man in the business delegation added.

"Oh…" Cassidy said, willing herself to focus on her job. *Pretend he's not there,* she told herself. *He's probably not there. You forgot lunch, after all. It's probably a hallucination brought on by hunger.*

"What I meant to, ah, say, was…" Cassidy began.

It's not him. It can't be him. It must be someone who looks like him. The world has no shortage of tall, dark and handsome. Just a look-alike, that's all.

"What I meant to say," Cassidy repeated firmly, "was that Europeans *will* be shocked and stunned—that it's not even *more* racy." She pushed out a laugh.

Luckily, the company reps laughed, also, letting Cassidy off the hook.

Off the hook in here, at least, Cassidy thought. *But I have to leave this room eventually.* And even though she warned herself not to, she peered out the glass one more time.

Eric Barnes still stood, with a patience she knew full well he had.

Cassidy looked away from him again. She would not allow this.

Her cell jingled. "Maxwell," she answered, willing her voice not to shake. She turned to face the wall behind her.

The voice on the other end sounded very close, because it was—the front desk was only steps from the room. "There's a man here to see you. Eric Barnes. He says he doesn't have an appointment but insists he see you. He says he knows you personally. I told him you were very busy, and I'd see what I could do."

Run, was her first instinct. Run out the back door. Keep running…

Cassidy sighed and rubbed her left temple. She had a roomful of people behind her and one of the most respected politicians in all of Europe counting on her. Running was not an option right now.

"I don't know when I'll be finished here," she said into the phone. "I'm waiting on the ambassador. But tell Mr.—Mr. Barnes that he can wait if he wants."

She clicked off and suddenly felt like Dead Woman Walking.

She turned to the group and talked some more, laughed a bit, and checked her watch often because every time she did, she forgot. She rolled her chair back a couple of inches, putting a blond man directly between her and her view of the lobby. By the time the ambassador strode in and the group rose in greeting, there were hot, damp patches under her arms and a thin rivulet of perspiration was snaking its way along her hairline.

"I apologize for my delay," the ambassador said. "But I am sure Cassidy kept you all as busy as she keeps me."

As the people in the room happily chimed in about Cassidy's helpfulness, the ambassador smiled at her. She tried to smile back, but felt an ugly grimace distort her cheek muscles instead. Before her boss could catch on, she stepped with great reluctance from the room, took a deep breath and took several heel-clacking strides to the lobby.

Eric had taken a seat, but he glanced up when she walked in and rose to his feet. Cassidy nodded at the reception desk, then walked right up to him and angled her head toward the door. He followed her outside and when she stopped and turned, he was suddenly so close that she had to tilt her head up a few inches to look at him.

A deep crease bisected the space between his thick, dark eyebrows—something that wasn't there before. His hair was different, and she realized with a start that it was shot through with gray. When had that begun? Gray hair seemed like something reserved for older men, much older men, who'd seen—but then, how could she presume to know what Eric had or hadn't seen?

He just kept standing there, silent, obligating her to speak first.

Questions began to throb across Cassidy's mind. *Why are you here? Why, after all this time? Why couldn't you just let go? Why are you making me face you now?*

But she finally chose to say only one word, and it came out of her throat in a ragged whisper. "Why?"

Eric recoiled. Not physically, but something in his

expression pulled back for a moment. Cassidy was unsettled by it; she'd never surprised him before.

"'Why?'" he repeated in a voice that was a bit lower, a bit harsher, than she'd ever heard it. "Did you just ask me, 'Why'? Why in hell are you asking me why? It should be me asking you. Why, Cassidy?"

Hearing her name in his voice again almost made her break down in sobs, but she fought hard against herself.

She wondered if he really thought she would answer him. Didn't he realize that if she could tell him why, years ago, she wouldn't have run? Couldn't he guess the betrayal she was hiding was more than he could bear?

She parted her lips, sticky with the remains of unrefreshed Chanel lipstick.

Maybe she would have said something. Probably not.

But she'd never find out for sure. Because at that moment, Eric reached out one hand, put it on the back of her head, pulled her close and covered her mouth with his.

It was as though he'd been in prison for ten years, for a crime he didn't realize he'd committed, and was finally tasting the sun again.

Cassidy's mouth was rigid and her glittering amber eyes were in a wide-open stare. Eric closed his eyes and brought both hands to her face, relaxing the smooth skin beneath his fingers, caressing her small earlobes.

He felt her resolve soften, along with her mouth. He nibbled gently with his teeth, and when her lips opened, he touched just the tip of her tongue with his. Someone made a moaning sound, and he couldn't tell who.

He leaned her against the wall, pressing his lower body against hers.

Then he felt another pressure. On his shoulders. Two hands. Pushing him roughly away.

He let go of her and stumbled three steps back.

Cassidy's face blazed as red as the highlights in her long, thick hair. She was breathing hard, her nostrils flaring like a prodded bull.

Another woman would have cried, "What are you doing, kissing me at the main door of the U.S. embassy, for crying out loud! I work here! And who do you think you are, kissing me like that, touching me like that? Get the hell away from me!"

But this was Cassidy, whose wordless emotions were always written all over her face. Eric flinched as if she *had* actually spoken.

He also flinched from the strength of his memory. Those three memories he never let himself remember?

Well, the first one smashed into him now. Hard.

Cassidy, glowing with new beauty at her Sweet Sixteen party. She coaxed him into the hall, away from her giggly girlfriends and clearly hopeful male friends. "It's my birthday," she said. "But I have a present for you. Happy birthday to me." Then she kissed him. An immature, inexperienced kiss. She looped her arms around his shoulders, touched his neck, and he felt her fingers trembling.

Their first kiss. And their last kiss.

Until now. His mouth still felt hers.

"Cassidy," Eric said. "I—"

She turned to walk away from him.

"Cassidy, please," Eric said. "I didn't come here for that. I didn't mean for that to happen. It just—I saw you and it just—it did. I'm sorry."

She looked at her arm where he grasped it. He let go and she looked into his face.

"I didn't even come here for me," Eric said.

Cassidy raised one thin, arched brow. He remembered when she learned how to do that in fifth grade. She'd given raised-brow questioning looks to people for three days, thrilled at her new form of expression.

"I came here for Professor Gilbert Harrison."

Cassidy did look genuinely confused then. She probably hadn't heard the teacher's name in ten years, Eric thought. She'd not only left him behind, she'd left everyone.

"I know you're at work," Eric said. "And I'm sorry to track you down here. I didn't know where you live and I needed to find you. Will you talk to me later? There's things I have to fill you in on."

Cassidy appeared to really want to shake her head no.

"Please," Eric said. "I came all this way. Gilbert really needs your help. He called a bunch of your old friends, and they want you to help, too."

"He didn't call *me*."

"No," Eric conceded. He *had* wondered why Gilbert hadn't called Cassidy, his former work-study student, who'd spent so much time with him and admired him so much. But Gilbert had said on the phone that he didn't want Cassidy to have to make the long journey back to the United States. On the other hand, a bunch of Saunders grads—particularly Ella Gardner, were positive Cassidy would drop everything and run back. Eric had run into Ella recently in Boston. She was the one who told him about Gilbert's predicament, and suggested Eric fetch Cassidy. She also asked him about the "crush" she'd suspected he'd had on Cassidy at Saunders. Eric would have laughed at the gross understatement if it hadn't been his own tragedy.

"No," Eric repeated. "But your friends insisted you should be found. And I guess I really had to agree."

Cassidy glanced behind her at the main door, either concerned she should be working—or searching for a place to flee.

"What time do you finish for the day?"

Cassidy glanced behind again.

"What time, Cassidy? I'll meet you here."

He wasn't going to let her leave without responding. She figured that out, because she said, "Seven."

"Seven?"

"Usually—but tonight, I have—"

"I'll meet you right here at seven."

She nodded.

A part of him longed to just stand in awe of her, gaping at the beauty she'd matured into. The girl he'd remembered wasn't even as beautiful.

But the other part of him, the part that had kept him awake for days and weeks and months on end, that distrustful part of him, made him say, "You won't be here at seven, will you? You're going to make me chase you, which is the only thing my pride has managed to stop me from doing."

Cassidy blinked very slowly, translucent lids covering and uncovering two golden lights.

Then she turned on her heel, yanked on the main door and disappeared into the building.

Eric stared at the spot she'd just vacated. A whiff of unfamiliar perfume lingered in her wake, a scent he'd already begun to miss.

His heart ached with emptiness. "That went well," he said to the wall.

Chapter Three

"Ambassador?"

Alan Cole looked up from his desk with a pleasant smile, a smile that came easily even though he'd been running around today longer than Cassidy herself had. "Yes?"

Cassidy handed him a few e-mail printouts. "You may want to take a look at these today. I'm leaving now, so..."

The ambassador pulled up the sleeve of his suit jacket, checked his gold watch and frowned. "I'm not sure about this..."

Cassidy hurriedly added, "Unless you need me to stay, of course. It's not necessary for me to leave now. Never mind, I'll just be in my office."

"That's right. According to my calculations, you've only put in a thirteen-hour day."

The shock of earlier events slowed Cassidy's ability to recognize the joke. She had turned all the way around to leave before she realized it, and then she turned back to the ambassador, who was fixing her with a shrewd look.

"Actually," he said, "I very highly recommend you do leave. Your day started before dawn. Anyone else would be long gone." He smiled again. "Anyone but the determined Ms. Maxwell."

Cassidy relaxed a bit.

Ambassador Cole was an admirable figure, both politically and as one of London's most eligible bachelors. His wife had died of breast cancer seven years prior, and Cassidy, who had been a junior staffer then, had sadly watched his heart breaking, along with the rest of the embassy. After that, the ambassador had dedicated his whole waking life to his work, and established himself as an influential voice for the United States in Great Britain. About a year ago, he had become fodder for tabloid speculation after he was seen with a stunning middle-aged blonde at an opera opening. The blonde turned out to be only a cousin, but society reporters persisted in their interest in the attractive politician, making it obvious they felt they'd kept their respectable distance long enough.

Alan Cole had short, graying-brown hair and deep laugh lines around his mouth and eyes. His smile was bright white and frequent. His racquetball habit—or, Cassidy often teased him, his racquetball obsession—kept his physical form trim, and his taste in suits was impeccable, assisted by the best tailors in the city. Despite being in his mid-fifties, he'd unwittingly made BBC News fans out of many young twentysomething women who might have instead been watching *"Coupling"* or *"EastEnders."*

The well-spoken and persuasive ambassador continually made an impression on world leaders and pundits alike, and after marveling at his obvious charisma for years, Cassidy was amazed when he took notice of her abilities and eventually promoted her to the position of his closest assistant. She strongly felt that one of her greatest professional achievements was earning his respect, and one of her most rewarding personal achievements was that he treated her like a member of his family.

Which was why she was one of the very small handful privy to the existence of his new girlfriend, a lovely watercolor artist who lived in Brighton, near the ambassador's summer cottage.

"And if I'm not mistaken," the ambassador now added meaningfully, "I often encourage you to leave at a decent hour, but you never do. I'm quite surprised at your sudden reasonable behavior."

Cassidy wasn't sure what to say. It had been bad enough that Eric Barnes had showed up after ten years to kiss her at the entrance to the U.S. embassy. She didn't want to call any more attention to herself. And she knew if she made something up, the man in front of her would not be fooled.

"I hope it's because you'd like some extra time to get ready for the party tonight," he said.

Cassidy was relieved at the out he'd accidentally given her. "Actually, yes. I was thinking of getting my hair done."

"Brilliant. I worry about you sometimes, Cassidy. Don't get me wrong. You're one of my best assets here, and I certainly wouldn't want you not to be, but you're maybe a bit too much of a—workaholic?"

Cassidy had to laugh. "*You're* telling me *I'm* a workaholic?"

"Okay, okay. I admit that is the pot calling the kettle…et cetera. But once in a while—" he paused to sigh significantly "—I see you flying around here, and I wonder if…you're trying to prove something. I hope it's not to me. You know I'm confident in your abilities."

"I know, Ambassador, and I'm appreciative—"

He cut her off. "Don't be. You earned it. But—" He paused, watching her for a sign to stop. Cassidy carefully kept her expression neutral, so he went on. "Maybe you're trying to prove something to yourself."

Cassidy blinked but didn't answer.

"I know what it looks like, you know," the ambassador said. "When Natalie died, I pushed myself and pushed myself, determined to prove to myself that I could go on, that I could handle life. You know what? It turned out I was right. I *was* capable of handling it, but I really didn't need to make my own life so frenetic to learn that lesson. It only made things harder."

Cassidy still didn't say anything.

"I want you to know that you can talk to me. If you

need anything, if you ever need a day or a week off, just say the word. We'd have a tough time without you, but we'd manage for your sake."

"I don't understand why this is coming up now," Cassidy said slowly, realizing that her mind had been screaming the same thing earlier when Eric appeared out of nowhere. *Why now? Why now? Can't you leave me alone...*

"Like I said, I have worried about you at times in the past. It's the expression on your face sometimes, a clenched-jawed, gritty look. I saw it again a little earlier today. I'm glad you're knocking off early. I want you to have fun."

Cassidy nodded.

"I mean it. Don't have little chats with the kitchen staff about the pâté, don't make sure all the serving trays are full, don't go into the bathroom to check the toilet paper supply."

Cassidy raised a brow.

"You didn't know I'm aware you do that, did you?" The ambassador laughed. "If you don't have fun tonight, you're fired. And that's that."

Cassidy smiled, the first genuine one she'd squeezed out in the last few hours. She knew Ambassador Cole's mind was weighed down with very serious things these days, not the least of which was his recent Northern Ireland peace initiative. He had other things to occupy him other than the mental state of his assistant, but here he was, insisting on addressing it.

She wasn't sure how she would oblige him, however.

Considering the day's events, fun was the last thing she'd be capable of. She felt her smile fade.

"Yes, sir," she said, and turned to go.

"Cassidy?"

She stopped.

"Are you all right?"

Tears threatened and she tilted her head up to the ceiling to try to make them fall back into the corners of her eyes. "You just asked me that, Ambassador."

"Not quite. I implied it, but that makes it easy for you to avoid answering, and I'd quite like it if you did."

Cassidy kept her back to her boss, because she didn't tell lies often and she was about to tell the biggest one ever. She squared her shoulders and brought her head down again. "I'm the same as yesterday. Just fine."

He didn't respond, so she added, with purposeful good cheer, "But I appreciate your concern. I'll see you this evening."

"Goodbye, Cassidy."

His words were simple but Cassidy recognized the tone. It was the pensive, analytical one he used when asked on television about things such as his opinion on America's foreign policies. He would answer clearly but his tone always implied hours of previous contemplation.

Cassidy left the room before the ambassador could contemplate her and her problems any longer.

Cassidy hoisted her weighty leather briefcase more securely onto her slight shoulder, pushed open the front doors and commenced a brisk pace. If fleeing the embassy at a run wouldn't have aroused certain suspicion, Cassidy might have done so—just flung her bag and three-inch-heeled boots onto the grass and sprinted off as fast as her black cashmere socks would allow. But she knew that subtle was better. The conversation with the ambassador had slowed her down a little bit as it was. She didn't want to take the chance of Eric showing up early and seeing her run from him—again.

No, she kept her pace quick but casual, glancing out the corners of her eyes, searching for any motion coming her way. Nothing. She let herself turn her head only once to look back, and Eric was not behind her. Her gaze traveled up the walls of the massive embassy, to where the immense golden eagle perched in a permanent moment of taking flight. Cassidy remembered the first time she had seen the bird, the symbol for the American idea of freedom. Every time since that first day, she'd walked into that building under the eagle's protective gaze, safe in her own freedom from Saunders, from the worst mistakes she'd ever made. Now, today, with no warning, the eagle, as imposing as it was, had proved itself unable to protect Cassidy from her past.

She should have known. And perhaps, in the back of her mind, she always had. Which was why she'd trained herself to stop thinking, stop dwelling, and just work hard.

It was crumbling now, the fortress she'd constructed around her mind and around the warm core of soft feelings deep inside her chest. She faced front again and shivered under her burgundy trench coat. She looked across expansive Grosvenor Square and caught a glimpse of the statue of Franklin D. Roosevelt before turning and heading up to Oxford Street.

A picture of Eric filled her mind and, for the first time, it was not a picture of Eric as a college graduate, an enthusiastic teaching assistant lecturing to an entire class but sending a secret signal through his hypnotic eyes to Cassidy and Cassidy alone.

It was a picture of the Eric she'd never seen before today, and hadn't wanted to ever see. Eric the man, the man with gray in his hair, the man experienced at having his heart torn in two by the woman he loved.

No. Cassidy gritted her teeth. Something else, something else. Franklin D. Roosevelt. She tried to fill her head with historical facts to shove out the sad picture. FDR. New Deal. Was that him? The New Deal. The New Deal was… She couldn't remember. She couldn't believe that she couldn't remember. Her memory was not normally a flawed one. He shot bears. Didn't he? And then—no. Crap. That was Teddy Roosevelt. Because of teddy bear. Right? Right? Was she remembering any of this right?

She turned a left, taking her past the famous Selfridges' storefront. Oxford Street was the usual tourist zoo and as she weaved in and out between clueless people clutching Underground maps, she let out a breath she didn't realize she had been holding. In this rush-hour crowd, no one would ever notice one woman in a dark coat carrying a briefcase. She whipped a wrinkled white diaphanous scarf from one pocket and tied it around her hair, binding up her one distinctive trait the best she could. For the first time ever, she wished it already was the middle of a bitter London winter, so she could conceal herself in a hat and muffler.

Why, Cassidy? Eric's broken voice bounced off the walls of her skull, reverberating over and over again. *Why, Cassidy?*

Why, Cassidy, she heard again, and this voice was ugly, sneering, triumphantly lecherous. Randall Greene. *I had no idea you would be as good as you looked. Virgins hardly ever are, you know?*

Cassidy strangled a sob back down her throat and forced her feet to go faster, slamming her heels so hard into the concrete that her shins ached.

"Go away, Eric," Cassidy said out loud, not caring if it elicited strange looks from the pedestrians hurrying beside her. The Bond Street Tube station was only one block off. She matched her chant to her steps. "Go away, go away, go away."

London was *her* city. She belonged here. Eric would leave. He had to.

Right. Franklin D. Roosevelt. Roosevelt was elected president in the year…

She glanced up at the street sign and froze. Someone slammed into her from behind, then roughly pushed around her, cursing her over his shoulder.

Cassidy stared wide-eyed at the sign. Gilbert Street.

Had she seen this before? Had her mind never made the connection to her old professor and friend?

She clenched her fists inside her pockets, angry at everything, angry at her city for failing to be her safe haven forever.

She knew, she just knew, that her no-thinking method couldn't save her from herself anymore.

She broke into a run, blindly shoving at down parkas and shopping bags, and slipped underground.

When Cassidy broke into an unexpected sprint, Eric cursed and quickened his pace as fast as he could considering the foot traffic. The line at the Tube ticket window was dozens deep, and Cassidy slipped through the turnstile, likely with some sort of commuter pass. Luckily, Eric had anticipated Cassidy's bolting from him and buying Tube tokens ahead of time was one of his preparations. The subway was sliding into the station just as Cassidy reached the platform, and with a bit of crowd-maneuvering, Eric managed to position himself behind her in the same car, where she'd have to turn her whole body around to see him. She didn't, though she definitely appeared to have a case of nerves, judging by her white fingers gripping the metal pole and the way she brushed a stray invisible strand of hair from her eyes over and over.

Good, Eric thought with defiance. Good. He'd suffered grief for such a long time. Inciting an attack of nerves on the woman he'd loved was at least some kind of weak revenge.

He was so busy watching her, and watching the way she glided toward the door three stops later at Holborn, that he almost didn't follow her. He leaped out at the last minute, just as a loud automated voice warned him and other passengers, "Mind the gap!" He straightened, afraid that his display of stupidity had alerted her to his presence, but she was already off and running.

They emerged, not quite together, into London's early evening. The streets were quieter in this neighborhood, and Eric had to drop back about a block and a half to continue trailing her. The buildings had brownstone fronts with varying doors—some high-polished blond wood, some functional dark brown, some with chipping paint and tarnished knobs. They reminded Eric of Boston.

Boston. Where he should be right now, working, and not halfway around the world, chasing someone who didn't want to be caught.

Cassidy abruptly turned and headed up the steps of a corner building. Eric quickly sidestepped into the doorway of a small Italian pastry shop. The scent of cannoli filled his nostrils as he watched her pull a pile of keys from her pocket and peer over her shoulder once before letting herself in.

Eric went into the shop and bought a cappuccino, staring out the large window at the building Cassidy had just entered. He stepped outside with his steaming cup, taking his eyes off the building's door just every now and then to study the unfolded London street map he'd picked up at the airport. He determined he was in the Bloomsbury section of the city. He mentally drew the route he'd have to take back to his hotel. After about twenty minutes he strolled over to Cassidy's building, sat on the top step and waited.

He wouldn't ring for her, because it would be much

too easy for Cassidy to refuse to let him in. Better for him to wait. She'd started to say she had something going on tonight. Provided it took her outside her home, he'd just surprise her on her stoop and have his little chat with her then.

She'd made it pretty clear she hadn't intended to keep their date at seven. And it was pretty obvious that if she'd hung around late, Eric would wait at the embassy as long as necessary. He had to hand it to her. She did make the better call, leaving early. She did her best.

But Eric had been blindsided that day she'd left him forever. Today, he could keep up with her, because he had more of an idea what Cassidy was all about. And that was her misfortune.

Because he was going to talk to her.

And in the hours between when Cassidy had stalked away from him and when he followed her home, he'd tried to decide whether he was going to make her talk to him.

He'd come here for Gilbert.

And he'd come here for himself.

But Gilbert was the one in a dire situation. Eric merely wanted an explanation for a long-ago wrong. Was it right to cross-examine Cassidy about her running away if it resulted in her refusal to come back to help the embattled professor, who really needed her?

Could Eric be so selfish? Gilbert had always been a confidant and mentor, not just to him, but to so many at Saunders.

No. On that stoop, with the cold concrete chilling his

butt through his suit pants, Eric made up his mind. He would talk to her about Gilbert, and only Gilbert.

She wouldn't have to talk back. About anything. She could just pack a suitcase, and he could just escort her over the ocean back to Massachusetts. Then *he'd* walk away from *her* and go on with his life.

Yes.

He glanced at the sky and tried to discern whether the darkening was due to nightfall or rain clouds. He hoped it was the former. Europe had greeted him early this morning with a depressing, driving rain. Eric turned his head and his gaze landed on a vertical row of doorbells. He was about to idly check for Cassidy's name when he snapped his head around to face the street again.

It hadn't occurred to him at any point—when he'd notified his political contacts he was taking a few days off, while he packed his suitcase, during the long plane journey—that Cassidy might not live alone.

There might be a man in there, who'd been waiting for Cassidy to return home. A man she was cooking dinner with. A man she was telling about her day—leaving out the part about seeing an old not-quite-boyfriend?

Was she kissing this man, so soon after—?

Eric set his jaw. Who cared?

Ah, crap. He leaped to his feet and scanned the doorbells. It was the top one of three: C. Maxwell.

No name crammed in next to hers in the small space.

Of course, it didn't mean she didn't have a boyfriend who lived elsewhere. For the time being.

Okay. He sat again and the step was no warmer for

his having just left it. He didn't know about her love life, and he wouldn't know. She certainly wouldn't volunteer it, and he wouldn't ask.

That kiss—why had he kissed her? With his careless spilling of emotion, he'd lost all leverage he'd had to be able to interrogate her, to finally learn the truth.

But that kiss—how could he have *not* kissed her? He'd tasted a memory of crayons and Play-Doh mixed with the exotic newness of her as an adult who craved a different sort of satisfaction. He couldn't get her off his skin. Shaking her off had been a challenging, sorrowful, arduous process, and now he was back to square one.

He sat there, at square one, shaking his head, for an hour and a half.

He was still sitting when Cassidy finally emerged. She didn't see him. She backed out of her front door, fumbling with her keys. A black trench coat was draped over her arm, implying she was in such a rush that it would be thrown on while walking quickly to wherever she was going.

She snapped open a little gold-beaded purse and dropped her keys inside. There couldn't be room in there for much else. She turned just as Eric got to his feet on the top step. She froze, her expression a blend of nervousness and extreme pissed-off-ness. She put her hand back on the doorknob.

"No, please," Eric said. "Please, Cassidy. I needed to talk to you. I knew you wouldn't meet me."

Cassidy blew out a hard breath, and her eyes narrowed. But Eric's eyes traveled down from her face, and her warning signs became insignificant. Her body—the body he'd once hugged through a navy Saunders University sweatshirt and denim shorts—was poured into a dress that rendered him speechless. Her freckled shoulders and arms were bare except for two thin straps. Her breasts, only slightly more cream-colored than the satin gown, swelled out from a tight bodice. The dress fell from her waist in gauzy layers, cut on a diagonal so that he had an unobstructed view of one long, toned calf. Bright red toenails peeked out from complicated-looking gold sandals, the kind a Roman goddess might have worn.

He dragged his gaze back to her face, framed with sleek burnished waves. Surprise was all over that flawless face. How could that be? How could she not know that if he'd loved her girlish looks, her womanly beauty could very well strike him dead where he stood?

"Give me a break," he said, but his words sounded, even to him, more of a desperate plea than a command. He added, "I came all the way here."

Cassidy spoke. "So I see."

"I mean, I came all the way to London, not all the way to your apartment. Though I did come here…I'm not stalking you."

Cassidy hesitated, panic spreading across her features. She shivered and shrugged into her coat. Then she raised her arm and, at a volume Eric had never heard come from her throat, yelled, "Taxi!"

She started down the steps. Eric took light hold of her wrist.

"What are you doing? You can't spare me a minute of time?"

Cassidy thought it over.

"Yeah, okay. I followed you. But I really have to talk to you and I didn't know how else to get through to you."

He squeezed his fingers around her skin a tiny bit, a physical entreaty.

"Hear me out. Just hear me out. You don't have to—" He cut himself off. She was regarding him warily, but she didn't yell for a taxi again. He let go of her wrist and dragged his hands through his hair, digging his short nails into his scalp. "You don't have to say anything. All right? I was wrong. I was wrong to ask you anything about why you—about why you left. I was wrong to kiss you like that. I was wrong to demand anything. It doesn't matter now. How could it matter now?"

Cassidy didn't answer, but Eric hadn't expected her to.

"It doesn't. That's not why I'm supposed to be here, it's not why I'm supposed to talk to you. I'm here for Gilbert Harrison, and Gilbert Harrison only. Can we go somewhere? Twenty minutes, I promise. Then you can go—wherever you're going. Unless—" shoot "—you have a date picking you up?"

Cassidy shook her head, a tiny motion that made Eric breathe a little bit easier.

"All right, then. Can we go somewhere for a drink, maybe?"

Cassidy pressed her lips together, thinking, then nodded vaguely to the other side of the street.

"After you," Eric said.

Cassidy nodded like a queen, then took the first step, wobbling the slightest bit on what could have been four-inch heels. Eric took her arm gently, hoping her stubbornness wouldn't make her shake it off so hard that she went sprawling onto the pavement.

She quietly allowed it.

They walked across the street and down about a half dozen doors to a pub called the Black Horse. He opened the heavy wooden door to a rowdy ruckus of football fans screaming at a TV above the bar. Eric couldn't tell whether the noise was happiness or disappointment. It occurred to him for the first time that sports fans tended to sound the same no matter who was winning.

When Cassidy, in her open coat, swept through the door that Eric held open, a collective hush fell over the men gathered around the television. The silence was only long enough to be noted, then catcalls and whistles filled the air. Eric tried to glare at each man in turn, but ale and sports had watered down any deference they might have had to a protective escort. Cassidy clicked by them, all but oblivious, leading Eric to a table in the back corner, and as soon as she was out of their eyeballing range, the noise level shot back up.

The waitress's cheerfulness was exaggerated by its proximity to Cassidy's sullenness. After she brought their beers, Eric leaned over and wiped Cassidy's side of the table with his cocktail napkin to avoid stains on the front of her beautiful dress. Cassidy watched him do it and waited to sip her beer until he took a drink of his own.

She touched a finger to her glass and swirled the tip in the condensation. Eric's jaw tightened while he tried to ignore the sensuousness of the movement. He resisted the urge to down half his pint in one gulp. Instead he sipped and cleared his throat.

"Gilbert is very close to losing his job," he began.

Whatever she expected him to say, that obviously wasn't it. Her jaw dropped. "What—whatever for?" she managed to ask.

"Just pure garbage. The new president of the board of directors, Alex Broadstreet, has it in for Gilbert, and it seems he's gotten the rest of the board to see things his way. They now all think Gilbert's too…well, old-fashioned. They don't like the way students have always been buddy-buddy with him. They think he should just stick to aloof professorial behavior, I suppose. They want him replaced."

Cassidy took another sip of her beer as the information sank in. "You can't fire someone for being a friend. There's more to it than that."

Eric liked how she was so sure of that, she stated it as indisputable fact.

"There is," he agreed. "The board's gotten wind of some—" he made quotation marks with his fingers "—'scheming' on Gilbert's part, and they don't like it one bit."

Cassidy, obviously baffled, made some noise that sounded like, "Huh?"

"Grade-changing. Helping at least one undeserving candidate get a scholarship—"

"That can't be right," Cassidy interrupted, and Eric raised his eyebrows. Cassidy didn't interrupt people. At least, she never had in the time he'd known her. Cassidy listened, waited for her turn to speak. Then there was usually a pause where she thought out her response. She never burst in with her verbal opinion. Perhaps this was a good sign. If she was outraged enough, maybe she'd agree to return with him.

"At any rate, the board is trying to have him discharged from his position, and it's apparent that they're attempting to do it as dishonorably as possible."

Cassidy shook her head with disgust. A flick of hair dropped over one eye. She brushed it away before Eric had to struggle against doing it for her.

"Then, before I left, I found out that Gilbert says he's been acting on behalf of a benefactor. Some rich, generous person committed to helping talented students who found themselves in bad situations.

"I don't know who this benefactor is," he went on. "He won't say. But Gilbert's called back a handful of Saunders alums, hoping that if he can show the board how successful they've all become, and how they've used their talents for the greater good, he might be able to save his job."

"He didn't call me," Cassidy said for the second time that day.

"No," Eric conceded. "But he told me he didn't want you to have to make the long trip back, that's all."

Cassidy was silent a long time. A long time even for Cassidy. When she spoke again, it was merely to repeat his last words. "That's all."

Eric was a little bit confused, but he shrugged it away. Today was emotionally confusing in about two million ways already. "I ran into Ella Gardner in Boston, where I work." He had a stab of realization that Cassidy didn't know anything about him anymore, and it saddened him a little. He added, "I'm an economist and political adviser."

Cassidy nodded, looking unsurprised. He had been a political science major and teaching assistant, after all. He was easily figured out.

"Um, yeah," he continued. "And so when I ran into Ella, she told me what was going on and how your former classmates all think you're needed back at Saunders. They remember how you were always there to lend a hand to anyone. They—missed you. They need you to testify for Gilbert, and I think you ought to use that sharp brain of yours to help them solve the mystery of the benefactor."

Cassidy had started shaking her head even before he finished speaking.

"What?" he demanded. "Don't tell me you won't. You were his work-study student. You were in his office all the time. You saw how students loved him, looked up to him. You saw—"

"I'm aware of what I saw," Cassidy said. Again with

the interrupting. She seemed to be fighting something inside herself.

"His wife died not too long ago. This job is everything to him. He needs support. He needs you." *I needed you, dammit,* he thought. *Where were you?*

Cassidy gazed over his shoulder at the football fracas. Eric stopped talking to increase the likelihood that she would speak.

He'd waited ten minutes and ordered another beer before she said, "I'll write a letter."

"You'll what?"

"A letter. To the board president."

"You'll write a letter?" *Are you kidding?* he wanted to shout. *I come all the way here after all this time, expose my heart to you, kiss you and this is all you're willing to do?* But he didn't say any of this out loud. Instead he went with, "I don't think that will be effective."

"But—"

Now it was Eric's turn to interrupt. "I've heard about this man, Broadstreet. I've heard how he has it in for Gilbert, and how heartless he is. You can write the most eloquent letter, Cassidy, of that I'm sure, but a letter is something he can drop on his desk and ignore. He's not easily swayed. The only thing that might help our case is walking in there and testifying in person. If it doesn't help with Broadstreet, it just might with the other people on the board."

"I can't."

"You can't what?"

Cassidy closed her mouth.

"You can't leave work? We can do it on a three-day weekend. You'll only have to take off one day, two tops." But she was shaking her head, so he tried again. "Is it the cost of the ticket? I can take care of it." She kept shaking her head, but harder. "I don't mind. Or I can lend you the money if that makes you feel better about it."

"No."

"Then what the hell is it? You have a dog that needs a sitter? A boyfriend you can't bear to leave behind for seventy-two hours?"

Cassidy set her jaw. "Neither."

"I'll get you a seat in first-class. You don't have to sit with me."

She resumed rubbing her finger on her glass. It made a squeaking sound. "I'm not going back there."

"Back where? To Saunders?"

She didn't answer, but she didn't shake her head, so Eric interpreted a yes. "Why not? You loved Saunders. You loved college more than anyone I ever met. You had a million friends. You were involved in a million activities—honor societies, tennis, tutoring. You never slowed down. You were happy and smiling and doing things all the time—"

"Stop." She literally covered her ears with shaking hands, like when she was a kid. He half expected her to say, "La, la, la," to drown him out. "I'm not going back there," she repeated, this time to the surface of the table.

He stared at her.

She had been a model Saunders student, the sort they tried to portray in catalogs and brochures to lure prospective freshmen. Her grades were A's across the board, in every subject. Hardly a day went by when she wasn't wearing her Saunders baseball cap. Eric couldn't walk the quad with her and have a conversation without students shouting, "Hey, Cassidy!"…"Cassidy, you'll be at the meeting later, right?"…"Cassie, can I borrow your math notes from this morning?" And Cassidy had waved and laughed with them all—

Except at the end. That last semester, when he'd hardly seen her. She'd been wan, drawn, slow-moving the few times he did. She said she was busy, lots of work, just this last push and she'd make it.

Now what was she saying? She wasn't going back there.

"Cassidy," he said, but her hands were still over her ears. He removed each hand gently and held them a moment. They still shook, very slightly. He looked down at them. The dim light in the pub obscured her freckles. Unless they weren't there anymore, faded away with time.

He didn't look at her face. He was afraid if he did, the directness would be too much for her. He ignored the promise he'd made to her at the beginning of the conversation. He had to. "Cassidy, what happened?"

She snatched her hands away.

"Something happened to you. Tell me what it was."

She stood abruptly. "I'm late."

Eric closed his eyes, took a deep breath and opened them again. "I know. I'm sorry."

He stood, also. She had one arm in her coat and was flailing her other arm around for the sleeve. He slipped behind her and held her coat. As her bare arm slid in, he said, "You look beautiful."

Cassidy whirled to face him, but she wasn't angry. She seemed close to tears. She blinked a few extra times.

"I guess you're going somewhere nice."

"A...a party." He smiled, and he didn't know what compelled her to clarify, "At the ambassador's home."

"I hope you have a terrific time," he said gently.

"I never have a—it's work."

He paused. "Work doesn't wear a dress like that."

Chapter Four

Now that her past had marched in, invaded her carefully constructed waking life, the only place for Cassidy to hide was the black dark of her bedroom.

She scrunched herself harder underneath the blankets, cold and shivering despite having cranked the heat up to a completely unaffordable level. She dug her heels into the mattress and felt the fitted sheet underneath her slide a bit. She sealed the top sheet over her head, entombing herself. Air dragged shallowly into her nose and mouth.

She hadn't done this in so long. Back then, that last semester at Saunders, bed was the only place she could bear to be, so she'd stayed there. The aftermath of her wisdom tooth extractions—four in one yank—had been an excruciating, swollen mess, but the painkillers had dulled it enough to let her sleep.

Then later, when the deeper, uglier pain came, the emotional nightmare of the worst mistakes of her life, she'd decided the medications could just as well dull that, too.

These memories had been locked away long ago, easily pushed aside with work. Until today, when Eric… And tonight, he told her she was beautiful, stared at her the way he used to. He'd held open the door for her and she'd thanked him, walked to the curb, hailed a cab and taken off.

She'd gone to the party and pasted on a smile for the ambassador, who she noticed glancing at her a few extra times. *I'm fine,* she let her smile say. *I'm fine.* The food was delectable, the wine perfect and the people charming. Cassidy couldn't wait to leave and come home.

To bed.

She clutched at the white sheet with both hands. Why did anyone ever get out of bed? It was satisfying just to lie there, letting sleep drift in and out like a friendly phantom, moving one finger at a time to see if they still listened to the brain, rolling over any time some new scenery was desired. Bed was the only place to be.

She'd adopted that philosophy suddenly back then, a complete turnaround from the rah-rah college girl she had been only weeks earlier. That rah-rah girl had completely ignored a toothache for months, knowing she hadn't long to go at Saunders, knowing she was so close to achieving a great job, a great life. She was aware in the back of her mind that the tooth was serious, but she didn't want to slow down. One morning she'd woken up with searing pain that stretched from her lips to her left ear, and broke down. The dentist said it was an infected wisdom tooth. They'd all need to come out anyway. Might as well get them all out at once. Cassidy agreed. Yeah, better in one pop. A weekend recovery, then—

It was no weekend recovery. The misery kept her out of class for more than a week. She refused help from her roommate, her friends, Eric, because she didn't want to be seen all puffy and red and achy. She'd fallen behind in her work, and having never fallen behind before, she had no idea how to handle it. So she handled it very badly. Which led to another mistake and another…

"Get on top, now," Randall said, breathing hard through his foul mouth. "That's a good girl. That deserves an A for effort…"

Cassidy wrapped her arms around her head and tried not to whimper.

Now Eric was asking her to go back to Saunders?

She empathized with Gilbert, her old professor and friend, who'd lost his wife, maybe soon his job. She remembered the day that altered their friendship. The day she found out his secret. It had nothing to do with her at all, yet she'd been so disappointed at him for being human.

Not long after, she'd become human herself, with her own grave errors, so now she understood him a little better, understood how everyone, no matter who, had the potential to mess up.

Gilbert didn't call her. Clearly he didn't want her to

come back. He was probably worried sick right now that she would. He knew Cassidy knew his secrets, but then, he had no idea that she had her own, more disgusting secrets that had nothing to do with him. He could rest easy when Eric returned and informed him she had no intention of ever stepping foot on the picturesque campus again.

She clenched her back teeth, her jaw trembling with the tension. The grinding molars hurt, reminding her of the pain, of the numbing painkillers, of the despair and desperation at falling behind that led her to abuse herself in ways beyond imagination.

Oh, Cassidy, Randall moaned in her memory. Cassidy pulled at her hair. *Cassidy, Cassidy...*

"Cassidy! Cassidy!"

"No," she said.

"Cassidy, wake up."

There was something in her hand. What was it? The phone? How did it get there? Her hair, staticky from rubbing under the sheets, crackled around her face and zapped her top lip. "What? Eric?"

"No, Cassidy, it's Ambassador Cole."

"What? Oh, oh." She shook her head and her magnetized hair stuck to her cheeks. "Ambassador? Am I late? What?" She looked at her alarm clock but without her contacts in, she couldn't read the glowing red digits. It was dark in her room.

"No, you're not late. I'm early, very, very early. Especially for a Saturday morning after a party."

Cassidy pulled the clock so close to her face, it touched her nose. Five-thirty? She went to work on Saturdays, but usually not until the early afternoon.

"War?" she asked, the first thing that popped into her thick, still-sleeping brain. She felt stupid when he laughed.

"No," he replied. "But I'm pleased to report the possible opposite. I got some news about the Northern Ireland peace initiative."

"What?"

"I'm informed that the opposing factions are taking the initiative seriously."

"They are?" The importance of what he was saying was weightier than her exhaustion and her eyes were suddenly wide open. "That's...that's..."

"That it is," he said. "At any rate, there's a lot of work to be done now. I need everyone on the diplomatic staff in today, early."

"I'll get everyone in by seven."

"Brilliant. You'll need to clear the schedule, and we'll plan a new one for the next few days, changeable at any time, of course, as events unfold. We'll hold a staff meeting at three today. That should be enough time for me to bring myself and everyone else up to speed. There's a few other people you need to call."

Cassidy snapped on a light, blinked hard and snatched a pen and pad of paper off her nightstand, kept there for just this kind of occasion. The ambassador talked and she wrote, her hand moving faster as adrenaline began to throb through her bloodstream.

The ambassador dictated the list of the duties Cassidy would have in his effort to change the course of current events.

In that possible history-book moment, Cassidy knew the ambassador unwittingly did one more thing, a small thing. He gave her a reason to get out of bed.

Eric sat in the small pastry shop, a scone on his plate, a hot tea in a mug on a table, a newspaper in his lap and Cassidy's building in his view.

He had gone back to the hotel last night. In the hotel, he'd flipped through unfamiliar TV channels and tried to follow shows he'd never seen, finally settling on a "*Seinfeld*" rerun. He couldn't laugh, though. There was nothing funny about anything.

He fell asleep shirtless, still wearing his suit pants. He awoke before the sun, but he didn't realize it until he pulled the heavy drapes open and found he couldn't see anything in the room any better than before. He realized, there in the morgue-quiet of predawn, that he might have seen Cassidy for the last time. What other reason had he to stay in London? He'd relayed the Saunders situation; she'd refused to come. Time for him to go.

But instead of packing his suitcase and checking out a day early, he changed into jeans and a sweater and left the hotel. He took the only Tube route he'd learned so far—the one to Cassidy's home.

Why, he couldn't say. Maybe just to see her one last time.

He dragged his eyes from the window and noticed the

paper in his lap. More specifically, he noticed an article that grabbed his attention and managed to hold it so well that he missed Cassidy leave her building, walk across the street and enter the shop.

He happened to lift his head and notice her at the same time she noticed him. Her mouth dropped open and she approached the table swiftly. He wondered if she intended to throw her steaming cup of something hot into his face.

"I didn't know you were coming in here, I swear," he rushed to say. "I had a good cappuccino here yesterday. I'm just a satisfied repeat customer. How could I know you'd come in here? You never liked coffee anyway."

"It's tea," she said evenly. She sat in the chair in front of him and regarded him, her face softened with some resignation. Then she gazed out the window, apparently lost in thought.

They sat together for several minutes without speaking. Cassidy took delicate sips of tea and Eric eventually ate his scone. He felt a wave of odd and unexpected comfort, as if they were a longtime couple, just having one of many breakfasts at one of their favorite places.

He tried to memorize her face. Again. To tide him over for the next ten years.

"Will you smile?" he blurted without forethought.

She looked taken aback.

"Just smile," he said. "Think of something nice and smile."

He could see her mind working, and after a few minutes of watching her strain, he jumped in.

"You're almost there," he told her. "Let me help you. How about...the frog?"

A long pause. Then she smiled. It was not a Cassidy-Maxwell-all-tooth special. It was shaky and weak, but it stuck.

"Atta girl," Eric said. "You remember?"

"Yeah," she said.

Eric smiled, too. He'd been around thirteen or so, and Cassidy's parents had taken him along on a day trip to Cassidy's cousins on Long Island. Playing by a little creek, he'd found a tiny frog. Having just seen a nature program about frogs, he took the opportunity to educate the younger kids about frog behavior. What he didn't remember exactly, he made up, because little kids didn't know any better. His know-it-all lecture was shot to hell when he lifted the little frog and it peed all over his hand before leaping away forever. Cassidy never remembered any of the impressive frog facts he'd told her, but always laughed at the memory of the "pissed"-off frog.

"You know, as a grown woman, you can't possibly think that's still funny," he said.

She nodded vigorously, her smile strengthening a bit. Then she sobered again. "I have to go."

"Again?"

"To work."

"At this hour? On the weekend?"

"Something's...come up."

"What?"

"I can't tell you that."

"Why? Is it a big state secret?"

She gave him a look. "I can't talk about it…"

"This state secret?" He held up the newspaper, the article that had captured his attention splashed on the front page.

Cassidy silently read the headline: Sides Mull Cole Peace Plan. She didn't know it had made the papers. The ambassador hadn't mentioned it.

"Here." Eric folded the paper and handed it to her. "You can read it on your commute."

"Thanks." She drained her cup and stood. She looked right into his eyes. "I—I'll be busy…"

"I would imagine so."

"So I won't—"

She didn't finish her sentence, but fervently hoped her meaning was clear, because it would hurt too much to say the words out aloud. *I won't be able to talk to you, or see you. It's time for you to go home.*

"I understand," Eric said.

Now that the shock of Eric's arrival had worn off, the idea that they were about to separate again felt unbearable. She couldn't comprehend this, because her life had been about escaping him, saving him from the truth of what she was. But letting go again was just as hard, even after all this time.

Cassidy did owe him one last thing and she decided she'd at least offer that up. She laid her hand across his on the table. It was warm and smooth, and she could feel his pulse beating under his skin. She said, "I'm sorry," but her voice choked on the word, so she repeated herself. "I'm sorry."

She stepped away from the table and walked out the door.

Sorry, she thought, walking fast, swiping at the tears that ripped down her cold cheeks. Whoever came up with "sorry"? Whoever thought one word would ever be enough to bandage up hurt, stem the bleeding from a wound too deep to ever heal right? That one word was all people had and they threw it around carelessly. The very same word was used if you spilled milk on someone's shirt. Sorry for spilling the milk. Sorry for ruining our lives. Sorry.

Sorry, Cassidy, Eric thought, *but "sorry" is not going to cut it.*

He'd come all the way here to get Cassidy. He had been about to leave without her.

But she had smiled.

If she could at least do that much, then he wasn't giving up so easily.

He walked up half a block, bought a phone card and dialed America from a public phone on the nearest corner.

"Both sides are currently considering the peace initiative I recently proposed," Ambassador Cole said in a loud voice, so that the staff members at the very back of the crammed-full room could hear him as well as Cassidy herself, who was seated at his immediate right.

She took copious notes as the ambassador outlined his needs from the staff for the next week or so, and the needs were many, considering he'd be out of commission on many current projects to focus specifically on this one right now. Despite the extra demands of work, the staff members' excitement was tangible. They were all aware of the time and effort that had been put into the ambassador's plan, and of the long-lasting effects it would have in the region if it succeeded. Though contact with major political figures and a firsthand view of world-changing events was pretty much a daily occurrence at the embassy, respect for the ambassador and what he was trying to do clearly had an impact on the psyches of the staff members.

Cassidy felt it herself, also, as an almost physical boost. With every word the ambassador said, he took her further and further away from the past twenty-four hours. Work could, and would, rescue her. She relied on it.

The ambassador said he'd met earlier in the day with all of the mission officers. He explained that the initiative would be undergoing revision. He didn't go into detail, but there were apparently some sticking points that would need to be hashed out. He said the State Department was sending several experts from Washington to consult closely with him to make those revisions, and that most of them were expected to arrive Monday morning.

"Fortunately," he said, "I can get to work right away because one highly recommended consultant happens to be in London on other business. He should be here shortly. I asked the desk to send him—ah, here he is now."

Cassidy looked up with the rest of the staff to see a man in a sharp, charcoal suit enter the room with his briefcase.

She squeezed her eyes shut. Oh, she did not get enough sleep last night. Lack of sleep never really bothered her before, but this was bad, because she could have sworn the man was Eric.

"This is Eric Barnes," the ambassador said, "He's an economist and political consultant based in Boston."

This is not happening, Cassidy thought. *This is just really not happening.*

"With Mr. Barnes already here in London, we can get a head start on the economic points in the initiative. Cassidy, will you please see to it that Mr. Barnes gets everything he needs?"

It seemed to Cassidy that Mr. Barnes had just arranged for everything he needed, quite without her help.

"Certainly, Ambassador," she said. She waited just one beat, not long enough for anyone in the room to suspect discomfort or animosity between them, but just enough to make Eric understand exactly how she felt about this development, and nodded once at him.

He nodded back, unsmiling.

She wanted to throw her pen right at his face. It was an expensive, blue silver-gilded pen from Tiffany, a gift to herself when she'd recently hit the big 3-0. But she would have gladly sacrificed the lovely pen for the pleasure of watching it smack him between his smug black eyes. The ambassador's presence in the room was the only reason she didn't.

She realized the ambassador was still speaking, and that she had missed maybe about a minute of it. Cursing herself for allowing Eric to distract her from her work, she began scribbling away again. This could very well be the most important event that had ever occurred during her time as office management specialist, and doing everything the ambassador needed her to do could make a difference in the peace initiative's success. She only turned her attention from her notes long enough to look at the ambassador, determined not to let Eric see her glance at him even once.

When the meeting was adjourned, Cassidy, uncharacteristically, was the first one out the door. She usually hung around after meetings to field questions or concerns from the staff, but she wanted to get out of the room quickly and breathe her own air in the quiet of her own office. If anyone asked, she could just claim she had a lot to do and wanted to get a jump on it.

She closed her door and dropped her face in her hands. Concentrate, she ordered herself. So Eric was here. So what?

There was a knock on her door. "Yes!" she called, swiftly stepping behind her desk and adopting her professional demeanor.

Eric opened her door and poked his head in. "May I?"

Cassidy sighed loudly and dramatically, dropping into her seat. It slid a little bit away from her, leaving her behind precariously perched on the edge of the chair. She lifted her hands, palm up, in a "Now what?" gesture.

Eric walked in and closed the door behind him. "We meet again," he said.

Cassidy's blood pressure built. She flexed her fingers in and out to keep her hands from curling into dangerous fists. How dare he act as though this was some happy coincidence and not something clearly orchestrated by him? "How?" she finally choked out, although she didn't really want to know.

"I called someone I know in the State Department, a former senator whose campaign I consulted on a few years back. It helped, of course, that I just happened to be here already."

Cassidy nodded, pressing her lips into a tight, grim line.

"This won't be so bad, will it?" he asked, smiling a little.

Cassidy wondered where she'd left her pen.

"I mean, this morning you sat with me at the café. Wasn't that nice? It seemed like your idea."

"That's because I *thought,*" Cassidy forced out, "that you were *leaving* the country today."

"Well, as it turns out, I'm not," Eric said, dropping the forced amiability but keeping his tone neutral.

"As it turns out," she repeated, with sarcasm.

They stared at each other, a prime example of what happens when an irresistible force hits an immovable object. Cassidy was determined not to budge, and it was clear Eric was just as determined not to stop pushing.

Finally, Eric turned to leave. When his hand touched the doorknob, Cassidy blurted, "I don't know what you're trying to accomplish..."

"Peace in Northern Ireland," he interrupted, turning back around. "Just like everyone else around here. Surely you'd agree that's bigger than the two of us."

Cassidy felt shame wash over her, a not unfamiliar

emotion. She looked down at the surface of her desk and nodded.

When she lifted her head again, Eric was gone.

Chapter Five

Cassidy wasn't accustomed to arriving to work early on a Sunday morning. Nor was she accustomed to seeing Eric standing at the front entrance when she got there.

He silently followed her through the lobby and into the front office, and might have followed her into her own office if she hadn't slammed the door shut behind her.

She sat at her desk, turned on her computer and lamp, and began to read several cables. She sent notices to the embassy sections that needed to respond to requests from Washington. After an hour of work, she peered out her large office window. The front office had filled up with staff working on assigned tasks, everyone appearing alert and bright considering they'd spent most of their weekend here.

She noticed Eric standing bewildered at a fax machine, squinting at the keys, trying to make something work. She watched him struggle for a few moments longer than necessary before emerging from her office.

She walked up to him and stood beside him as he punched buttons. The machine beeped angrily.

"I'm not doing something right," he finally said. "The one I usually use is different from this."

If Eric were anyone else, Cassidy would have assured him that this particular machine was a little dodgy and often needed a bit of expert prodding. But Eric was Eric, and Cassidy just mumbled, "I'll do it."

He stepped aside and let her handle it. When his document was sucked through and the okay message was in his hand, he said, "Thank you."

"I can't figure that machine out," she heard behind them, and turned. The ambassador was shaking his head. "Only Cassidy has the magic touch with it. I'm sorry, I neglected to formally introduce you after the meeting."

"No need," Eric said, and Cassidy stiffened. She could only imagine what was coming next. *I taught Cassidy how to ride a bike. I helped her build her baseball card collection. She was my student. She was supposed to be my girlfriend. Oh, and I kissed her. Yesterday. Right out there, in fact…*

"We were at Saunders University together," he merely said. Cassidy exhaled.

"Ah," Ambassador Cole said. "That's in Massachusetts?"

"Yes."

"Well, I suppose I don't have to waste time extolling Cassidy's intellectual virtues to you."

"No, sir."

"And I guess I don't have to sell Eric to you then, either, do I, Cassidy?" the ambassador asked.

"Uh," Cassidy said. She swallowed. "No."

The ambassador raised his brows, that disconcerting searching expression on his face.

She forced her mouth into a smile. "If it were up to me, I'd have handpicked him myself."

"That's good to hear. We're ready for you now," he said to Eric.

The two men left, leaving Cassidy to wonder how long revising a peace plan could take. She was only an hour into the first episode of "Eric at the Embassy" and she'd had enough.

Several hours later, while Cassidy was updating the ambassador's schedule, he popped his head in.

"Anything urgent?" he asked.

Cassidy gave him a scaled-down summary of the day. It wasn't much, being a Sunday, and none of it was as important as his current project.

"Right," he said as Cassidy resumed typing. "See you later. Oh, and one more thing."

"Yes?" She suspended her hands over the keyboard.

"Concerning Eric Barnes—"

Crap.

"I thought I detected a little tension. Is everything all right?"

"Of course."

"Because—"

"It's fine. Eric's an asset," she emphasized. "He has a fine mind."

"So far, I do agree with that assessment."

He left and Cassidy shook her head. Eric's fine mind, indeed. A scheming mind, more like. But those beautiful black eyes. And that body, which even under a suit still appeared to be as firm and strong and—

Ahem.

She was going to have to keep her volatile emotions in line and not create a distraction around here. Ambassador Cole was kind and a good friend to her to have noticed anything other than his work, but he should not have to.

Cassidy carried an extra stack of napkins from a supply closet and placed them next to the tower of paper plates. It was Monday, and the rest of the consultants had arrived from Washington. She'd been in charge of ordering in a catered lunch as a welcome to the embassy. She inhaled, sorely tempted to pick at something quickly before everyone filed in, but then the first person entered the room, and then another, and very quickly the space was full with eating and chatting.

She stood in a corner, surveying to make sure no one needed anything. Eric was one of the last to arrive. He picked up a plate and passed over the chicken in favor of the pasta, just as Cassidy knew he would.

He dropped a roll onto his plate and said something

to the woman next to him. She laughed. Cassidy frowned.

She was still frowning when Ambassador Cole came in, and when he glanced her way, she quickly rearranged her expression into a more pleasant one. The ambassador, all hospitality, worked his way around the room, and when he was standing close to Eric, Cassidy made a beeline.

"Eric," she said brightly. "Tell me, how's Boston treating you?"

Eric looked as stunned as if she'd asked him if he'd ever seen the Queen of England naked. He answered slowly. "It's fine. The T fare's gone up a few times, and the Sox finally won the series, but it's the same old city."

"I haven't been there in so long," Cassidy went on.

"Yeah, I'd say about ten years," he said.

The ambassador glanced at them. She smiled so hard at Eric, her eyebrows hurt.

"Still teaching at Saunders?" she asked.

Thankfully he played along. "No, I stopped teaching after you left. I went into politics full time. I had no reason to be there anymore."

She peeked at the ambassador to see if he'd heard Eric's last comment, but he was in a football discussion with several men.

"Speaking of Saunders," Eric said.

Do not start with the Gilbert Harrison thing. Not here, please, she silently begged.

"Do you remember," he asked, "the time there was a fire drill at your dorm in the middle of the night and for some reason they didn't let you guys back in for an hour? I happened to be studying at the library late that night, and people were milling around, waiting. I found you sitting on the grass in the quad in your robe and bunny slippers. At least it was a warm spring night. Remember?"

Cassidy blinked. Did she remember that? Yes…she did. "We went somewhere…to eat."

"Yup, we went to the twenty-four-hour diner up the street. And you were all worried that everyone there would look at you funny, out in your pajamas."

"But everyone was," Cassidy said, remembering. Lots of kids in her dorm had had the same idea they had. The twenty-four-hour diner that usually saw an occasional shift worker for coffee late at night transformed into a festive coed slumber party.

"That's right, everyone was. Except me. I was overdressed in my real clothes. I remember some girls had crazy green cream on their faces. Your robe was pink with little yellow flowers."

Cassidy blushed over his memory of that detail, but she realized she remembered little things, too. She remembered drinking a chocolate malted and eating a piece of cake. She remembered that one guy started singing "1999" by Prince, and they all joined in. She remembered walking home slowly with Eric at dawn. The dorm had long since opened, but no one had wanted to leave the diner until the morning light started breaking through and eight o'clock-classers realized they needed to shower and change into real clothes.

That had been her freshman year, and she and Eric

hadn't acknowledged their feelings yet. But she remembered he gave her hand a secret squeeze before leaving her at her dorm. She remembered he whistled as he'd walked across campus.

All of it came back to her right then. A memory she'd stored but hadn't pulled out in years. It was dusty now, but still colorful.

"That was a fun night," she said.

"Oh, yeah," he agreed. "One of hundreds of fun times."

Hundreds? Really? Hundreds of good Saunders memories?

Maybe…

"Reminiscing about the good college days?" the ambassador asked, cutting into her reverie.

Good old days, Cassidy scoffed in her mind. But then again, Eric had just reminded her of one good one. She twisted her lips.

"That's right," Eric said. "You know, even back then Cassidy showed a real penchant for politics."

"I'm not surprised. Political situations change daily, and Cassidy's always in the know. Sometimes before me," he said, winking.

"Ambassador," Cassidy said, "that's not true."

"I've just never admitted it before," he said, his eyes twinkling. Then he moved to talk to someone on their left.

Eric ate a forkful of pasta. She watched his mouth while he chewed, then realized she shouldn't. She looked at his eyes instead, but he was looking right back. She put her gaze firmly on his earlobe, which should have been fine, but the skin there seemed so soft and vulnerable, reminding her of how she used to whisper childish secrets to him—before she'd made the decision to tell no more.

Eric swallowed. "It doesn't surprise me that you're working here," he said. "It only surprised me that I had to find out from your mother years ago."

Cassidy sucked in a breath, then grabbed a roll off the table and stuffed it into her mouth. She mustered a false, closed-lipped smile and moved away from him.

It was dark in the front office when the diplomats filed out of the conference room to retrieve their coats and head back to their hotels. Dark, Eric noticed, except for the faint soft glow from one closed office.

Cassidy's office.

She'd tried to keep her distance from him since yesterday's lunch, but despite the size of the embassy building itself, they kept crossing paths. When they did, they acknowledged each other awkwardly and silently.

As the others headed for the door, Eric stepped a little closer to the office. He could see her profile, but he was careful to stay out of her peripheral vision.

The computer cast an eerie light on her face, paling her skin to a shade under translucent. Her wavy hair was tamed at her neck in a large black clip. She'd taken off her jacket and her black silky top looked almost as soft as her bare arms.

Eric felt his body tighten, a sensation that was all too familiar these past few days. He turned his head and saw the last person leave without looking back. He raised his hand and rapped lightly on her door.

She jumped a little and snapped her head around. He waved. She shook her head with something that was probably close to disgust, and opened the door.

"We meet again," she said.

"You've gotten kind of sarcastic in your old age, haven't you?" Eric asked, but not meanly.

"I'm not as old as you," Cassidy retorted, then appeared surprised at her own words.

"That's the spirit," he said. "Shouldn't you be at home?"

She nodded. He peeked over her shoulder at the computer. "Doing research?"

"Yes," she said.

He leaned over to better see the screen. "Recipes?" he asked.

"I'm not on the clock," she said defensively, "and it is for work."

"You're going to cook something? You can't cook. Uh," he said, "can you?"

She nodded in that proud, show-offy way Cassidy Maxwell had when she was good at something you weren't good at.

"That looks like a pretty elaborate dessert," he said. The picture was of a glass plate of colorful fruit, glazed to a delicious shine. "Are you making that for a party?"

"For here," she said, then added, "for a Friday treat."

"You do that often?"

She shrugged, and he interpreted it as a "Sometimes, when the mood strikes."

"That's very generous of you. Everyone must appreciate it."

She nodded.

He looked at the screen again. "Are those pears?"

"Yes."

"Remember the box of pears?"

She squinted.

"I had to remind you about the frog, I had to remind you about the diner slumber party, now I have to remind you about the pears?" he asked. "Woman, your memory is shot to hell. All right, I think I was about thirteen, so you were about eight. And my aunt in Florida sent us this box of pears."

He saw recognition flicker across her face. "Pears. Christmas."

"That's right. It was Christmas. And my mother showed you the pears and you laughed so hard. You said, 'Pears for a present! You get pears in the supermarket!'"

Her mouth promised a smile, but didn't deliver. Yet.

"And she said to you, 'Cassidy, these aren't just any pears. Try them.' So you grabbed the whole box and you ran to sit—"

"Under the tree." Her eyes widened. "I remember…"

"And you sat under the tree and you opened the box, and you grabbed a pear. You almost bit into it, but you stopped and gave me one first. And we bit into them at the same time. You were laughing, calling them tasty magic Christmas pears. Close your eyes."

Cassidy cocked her head to one side.

"Close your eyes now."

She obeyed. He didn't know why, but she did, and he was glad.

"Can you still taste those pears?" he asked. "Because I can. There was so much juice, it ran down our arms and we had to push up our sleeves. Then you licked your arms. You laughed like crazy. Then you licked mine."

He trailed a finger up her forearm. She started, but didn't open her eyes.

"Can you taste it?" he asked again. *I know you can. Trust me, Cassidy, and tell me you can. Tell me.*

"I—" she began. She licked her lips, moistening them to a sheen. Eric fought with himself not to touch them with his fingers, with his own lips.

"I can," she finally said. "I can." Her face contorted slightly with the effort of either the memory itself or the confession of it.

In a flash, Eric understood. He understood that while he'd spent the past ten years comforting and sustaining himself with their shared experiences, she'd spent the same amount of time blocking them out.

He just didn't understand why.

He dropped his hand to his side and she opened her eyes. They stared at each other. They both knew that, however briefly, she had just allowed him something. He willed her to be assured that it was safe, that she was safe.

His gaze traveled accidentally down to her chest, where he could see her tightened nipples pressing through the silk of her top. He quickly looked at her face again.

God help him. He would not cup her face in his hand,

pull her in for a kiss, lay her down over the desk, run his hands underneath that shirt and feel her burning underneath him.

Burn. She'd burned him before. He would get close to her again, find out her secrets, bring her home. That was his original goal and he was sticking to it.

Cassidy grabbed her jacket off her chair and put it on. "Have a good night," she said, signaling he should leave her office. He did, waiting just outside her door as she closed up.

She walked past him at a brisk pace and was on the sidewalk outside before he could blink. "Are you going home?"

"Why don't you follow me and find out?" she asked. Her words were meant to sound sharp, but her voice was thin and lacked any real anger.

"It's dark out."

She didn't slow her pace. He was almost out of breath. When he got home, he'd have to hit the gym more often. "It's night," she answered.

"Slow down, will you?"

She stopped. "What is it?"

"Just go at a normal pace, please, so I can chivalrously walk you to the Tube station."

She shook her head no.

"I know you don't need me to protect you, but…"

"You can't anyway."

"I can't what?"

She didn't answer.

"I can't what? Protect you?" he persisted. Still nothing.

She flinched. Something glittered in her eyes.

"When did I ever not protect you?" he asked. "I've been looking out for you every second for most of your existence. I never let anything hurt you."

Cassidy mumbled something that sounded suspiciously like, *Except myself.*

He used all his inner strength to stop himself from demanding an answer. There was no lasting point in shaking it out of her. If she could trust him again…

"It's getting cold," he said. He reached over and fastened the top button of her coat. It was a gesture he'd made a thousand times in the past. He felt her shiver. "Let's go. I'm not doing this for you. I'm doing it for me. It's not right to let a woman walk the city streets alone at night when you don't have to. Just ease my mind and do it. We're halfway there, anyhow."

They walked silently, but not together. Miles of space separated them. As they rounded the corner, a woman weighed down with boxes and bags from Selfridges tottered toward them. Eric tugged Cassidy close to him to let the woman pass. They kept walking and Cassidy didn't move away from him until they reached the station.

She faced him, clearly nervous, either at the emotions that had run back and forth between them or at what he might say next.

He decided to let her off the hook, just for the time being. "Good night, Cassidy. See you tomorrow. Thank you."

She toed the sidewalk with one boot. "Thank you," she repeated reluctantly, as if he'd said it to remind her of her manners. Maybe he had, subconsciously.

She headed underground and he watched her red head until distance and the dimness of the station swallowed it up.

Damn.

As a political consultant, part of Eric's job was to look at all angles of an issue, see how it would play out with all different kinds of voters. Maybe he should have applied the same theory to this situation.

He'd been hoping that renewed proximity to Cassidy would affect her. He hadn't counted on how it could affect him.

But it wouldn't. This wasn't about him. He wanted their shared memories to touch something in her, spur her to action. But he'd remain immune.

He jammed his hands into his coat pockets, shielding them against the wind that had suddenly picked up. Or maybe it was just that he felt the stinging chill more now that Cassidy wasn't by his side.

He headed back to his hotel room, which he anticipated would be just as cold.

On Friday afternoon, weary after a long day ending a harrowing week of mind-scraping work, Eric plugged in his laptop at an extra desk in the front office to check his e-mail.

And to write one.

To: Gilbert Harrison
From: Eric Barnes
Re: London calling

Wanted to check in to see how you're holding up and to explain my delay. By now I'm sure you've heard about Ambassador Alan Cole's peace initiative being considered by both sides in the Northern Ireland conflict. As I happened to be in the embassy area searching out Cassidy Maxwell, I volunteered to consult. It's a draining job but a rewarding and humbling one, and something I would have wanted to do even if I hadn't already been here.

I anticipate being home in less than a couple of weeks, and I hope to not be alone. Cassidy…

His fingers stilled after typing her name. He glanced up from the screen and saw her putting out little paper plates and forks. Ah, the Friday dessert. A couple of people asked her what the treat was, but she just shook her head, and said, "You know it's a surprise until you see it."

She said it with a smile, which Eric fixated on until she turned and went back into her office.

Cassidy…

He deleted her name slowly, letter by letter, and began the sentence again.

You can certainly be proud of Cassidy. She practically runs this place single-handed. The ambassador personally relies on her for everything. She's made her mark here, just as surely as she made her mark on the Saunders campus.

Should he tell Gilbert that Cassidy had dug in her heels, said she'd never show up at Saunders again?

Nah. That kind of thing was not likely to give a desperate man hope.

Cassidy emerged from her office, carrying the dessert—a huge dark chocolate cake. Eric shifted his focus from the cake to her face.

She was staring right at him.

He could easily discern what she was thinking. *See? Not a pear in sight.*

He waited until she was busy with her coworkers again before he allowed himself a quick grin. No pears meant he had gotten to her—a little bit.

Hang in there, Gilbert, he typed. I'll be back soon with a star witness in tow for you.

He added his contact information at the hotel and signed it, Your brother-in-arms, Eric. He hoped the sentiment would cheer the poor guy up.

Gilbert closed out the e-mail without replying.

It had made him feel worse than ever.

This "witness" would be a star, all right. One that would shine brightly enough to illuminate his mistakes for the world to see.

Chapter Six

Cassidy dashed from the shower on Sunday night, half clutching her damp robe around her in a futile attempt at warmth, to grab the ringing phone. "Yeah?" she said when she pressed it to her ear. "Uh, hello?" she amended.

"Hi, what's up?"

She held the receiver away from her face and stared at it. *Hi, what's up?* The voice sounded familiar, as if she'd heard it recently, but a tiny bit unfamiliar, as if when she'd heard it, it hadn't been over the phone wire.

When the caller's identity dawned on her a split second later, she collapsed on her sofa, despite dripping water all over the upholstery. She pressed the phone back to her face and laid her already sweating forehead in her free hand.

Her apartment phone never rang. Her cell phone was the one she relied on. The few times a week her home phone rang, it was only telemarketers or wrong numbers. Either would have been preferable to this.

"Cassidy," Eric said in her ear, "you need to say something. That's how a telephone works."

She hated personal phone calls. She far preferred communicating face-to-face. She needed a visual point of reference. Plus, people who liked to talk on the phone always expected you to say far more than would be necessary to carry on a conversation on the same topic in person.

She'd hated the phone for a long time—certainly long enough that Eric was damn well aware of it.

"How did you get this number?" she demanded.

"I'm doing fine, thanks for asking."

She wanted to hang up on him, but a tiny voice inside her told her to wait and find out what he wanted. Whatever it was, it would be better to deal with it in private here than to air it out at the embassy.

"I called Information," Eric continued. "You know, if you don't want anyone to call you, why don't you have an unlisted number?"

"Because, until now, I didn't know anyone in London well enough to avoid," Cassidy said.

Even though she hadn't meant it as a joke, Eric laughed. "Well, until now, *I* didn't know anyone in London well enough to call," he said between chuckles.

She was again tempted to hang up, but that little voice once more told her to wait. Wait and listen to that laugh, the one she'd successfully elicited almost every day of her childhood. The sound was just a little bit different than she'd remembered. It came from deeper in his throat now, making his amusement sound more sophisticated.

Ideas of other areas in which this new sophistication could also be residing made her squirm a little on the sofa. It reminded her that there were plenty of things she didn't know about this more mature Eric.

A lock of damp hair fell out of her towel turban and smacked her in the eye. She used one finger to push it back.

"So, what's up?"

"Cut to the bloody chase," she said. "What do you want?"

"Some friendly conversation."

Cassidy exhaled noisily through her nose, so her annoyance would be clear.

But Eric was undaunted. "Nothing deep or dark. Just a chat. Cable TV gets repetitive pretty quickly after an entire week."

Try it for ten years, she thought. Then again, for all she knew, he had.

"This hotel room is nice, but boring," he added. "Lonely."

Cassidy's mind unwillingly conjured up a picture of Eric reclining on the bed in his rumpled suit pants, shiny black shoes kicked off, one arm behind his head. In her mental picture, there was no phone, just his free hand crooking a finger at her, beckoning her.

Stop it now, Cassidy.

"There's no one else you could be talking to?" she asked, more for herself than for him. "No…woman?"

"Well, there is the lady at the lobby desk."

Cassidy felt an unfamiliar pang.

"And she does have a fantastic accent."

Another pang. She crinkled her nose.

"But she's about a hundred and ten years old."

Relief?

"I don't think she and I would have much in common," he added.

"Oh, and we do?"

"Of course we do. Lots. Those things didn't go away. You can't erase the past, right?"

She felt another pang, but this one she recognized quite well as her old pal Guilt.

There was another brief pause. "Don't you have a book to read or something?" she asked in desperation.

"Nope."

"There are lots of good bookshops in London," she pointed out. "Many still open at this hour."

"I have to confess, I've been too busy at work to read any book reviews or anything," he said. "I don't know what's out, or what's good. How about a suggestion?"

Oh, for God's sake. Fine. She'd play along if it meant he would hang up soon. In as few words as possible, she began to tell him about a history book she'd been reading about the French Revolution. He asked her a few questions, which she answered, which led to his saying he'd once read a similar book, which opened more discussion, which stretched to tangents. Soon they bounced from one topic to the next like a ball in a Ping-Pong tournament. Almost like old times.

"Cricket is not just a 'complicated and crazy form of baseball,'" Cassidy found herself saying at one point.

Eric's response was a disdainful snort.

"First," Cassidy insisted, "the games are only barely alike. Second, if anything, the rules are probably easier to grasp. You've never watched cricket in your life."

"Not for an extended period of time, no."

"Yet, interestingly, that doesn't stop you from forming an opinion on it," she said. "And, by the way, I hear this all coming from a guy who couldn't actually *play* baseball if his life depended on winning a game."

"You wound me. And besides, I have no idea what you're referring to."

"Remember when you were playing with a bunch of grad students and TAs at Saunders? You were covering third base, or rather, you were supposed to be."

"What?"

"The batter hit a grounder right to you. You just stood there. The ball whacked you in the shin."

"I fielded it," he argued. "Despite massive pain."

"Your throw to first was twenty minutes late."

"I was distracted."

"Uh-huh."

"By you."

Cassidy shut up.

"You had just arrived and sat down. Your books were next to you on the bench. You waved to me just as the ball was hit."

Had that been it? Maybe. "You had to ice your leg for a week," she said.

"You checked on me seventeen times a day. I didn't feel a thing."

Change the subject, change the subject, Cassidy commanded herself. Wait a minute. Baseball? How—and when—did they get onto this anyhow? She looked at the clock. Whoa. Very obviously wrong. Must have stopped earlier in the day. She crawled to the other side of the sofa and leaned way over to see into her kitchen. The wall clock confirmed the smaller one. They'd been talking nearly two hours.

Her throat was raspy.

"Good recall, by the way," Eric said. "I was beginning to think you'd been kidnapped and had your memory bank erased by an evil mastermind."

She wondered what Eric would say if she told him that mastermind had been herself.

But that memory *had* come to the surface far easier than the other ones he'd recently dredged up. The clarity of her young adulthood was fast returning.

Thanks to Eric.

Despite the tension of seriously unresolved issues, other feelings *were* still there between them.

There was a pause. Cassidy wondered what he was doing. Was he lying back against the pillows, staring at the ceiling? Was he remembering her back then, the innocent good girl who had adored him so much? Or was he thinking about her current self, the cantankerous and reluctant colleague?

Was he as confused as she was? Was he still as attracted as she was?

But—no, she wasn't.

Oh, yes, she was. That truth didn't surprise her, but it did terrify her.

That embassy kiss, still fresh on her lips despite the long days that had elapsed, had terrified her, also.

She pulled the towel off her head and threw it on the floor. Her hair fell around her shoulders in dried-out, knotted ropes.

"Nice to hear your voice, Cassidy."

The comment, usually a throwaway one between acquaintances, held more meaning here, and she got it.

Before she gave in to her urge to admit that to him, she realized he had already hung up.

The top of her navy bathrobe had drooped open, leaving her a bit chilled. She moved to close it, but stilled her hand in midair about four inches. She closed her eyes, concentrated on the air surrounding her body. She replayed Eric's new laugh in her mind and let it hover around her, swirl over the vulnerable bare skin of her chest, right over her heart.

Exposed.

It was—not terrible.

She pressed the dead phone receiver to a spot under her collarbone for just a moment before replacing it on the cradle and gathering her robe shut. She headed to the bathroom mirror, perversely grateful for the mess her hair was in. She needed the prolonged distraction to fill the short time before bed.

* * *

She wasn't sure what to say to Eric the next day at the embassy but, as it turned out, it was a problem she needn't have considered at all. She'd had an errand at the copy shop first thing in the morning and by the time she arrived, the ambassador and his advisers, including Eric, were already hours into meetings. When evening fell and Cassidy found herself alone in the front office, she told herself firmly that if she couldn't find a good work-related reason to hang around, she was going home.

An hour later, after online-ordering some *extra* extra staplers and rolls of Scotch tape, she took a fruitless look around for humanity, found none, and left with her jacket and briefcase.

She dug her gloves out of her pocket and put them on, wrapping one arm around herself. The TV meteorologists, whom Cassidy had long ago learned to ignore, had predicted unseasonably low temperatures this week and, for once, they seemed to have been on target. Too bad for her she'd picked today, of all days, to wear a skirt to work. She didn't do it often because her days were long and she found trousers more accommodating, but this morning she had just—felt like a change of wardrobe.

Out of nowhere. Funny.

Her kneecaps, having last been exposed in the summer, trembled against the cold air.

It wasn't the only part of her that ached. She could have sworn the inside of her mouth was rubbed raw from all that prolonged talking last night. She didn't know what had come over her. She decided to blame it on the phone. It made her forget her real self. She'd slipped into her confident, talky work self.

If the phone rings tonight, I'm not answering it. By the time she saw Eric tomorrow, enough time would have elapsed for both of them to forget that whole phone call altogether.

No, they wouldn't.

Maybe a subtle hint would be best. Nothing mean, just some way to convey that it had been nice to catch up with him, but it was best to keep it strictly business.

Ah. She had it.

She doubled back three blocks and darted into the nearest bookstore to the embassy. It was one that was open late, one she'd spent many hours of her alone time in over the years.

She wiggled her fingers at the shop owner as she entered, and he recognized her and nodded without comment. He was too wise to have conversations with customers. He seemed to understand his little store, with its old carpets and dim lights, was a haven for people searching out some quiet. Cassidy had now and then seen people enter chattering away happily, then falling to a hush before the door closed behind them. It was that kind of reverent place. Her own natural reticence was welcome here.

Cassidy headed to the aisle she frequented most, history and current events. Located so close to the embassy, the small shop stocked this section well and often. Cassidy could read a book review in the morning paper, stop by the store in the afternoon and find the book prominently displayed.

She rounded the corner of biographies and stopped in her tracks. She didn't even get the luxury of a moment to shake her head in disbelief, because her hard heels on the floor had made Eric raise his head and see her at the same time she saw him.

He seemed surprised this time, a welcome table-turning. But it was an honest coincidence. He couldn't have followed her *and* gotten here first.

"Wow," he said. He tilted up the book he'd been studying, and it was the one she'd recommended the night before, the one she'd come in to buy. "Guess we both had books on the brain," he said.

She wanted to just lie on the floor and stretch her arms wide and never get up. Why bother? Sometime in the last week, she'd lost all control over her life.

"Looking for something special?" Eric asked. She examined his face, finding nothing but friendly inquiry.

"Yeah," she said, pointing at his book. He shut it with a clap.

"This one?"

"Yeah—for you—"

"You were going to get it for me?"

She wished he hadn't sounded so grateful about it, as if it was going to be a thoughtful gift and not a big brush-off. It just made her feel guilty and bad.

"Well, no need, then," Eric said. "I just came to get it myself on your recommendation. Even though it's only in hardcover. That means I really—trust you."

His last two words sounded as if they'd slipped from his mouth before he could stop them, but he surged on. "I trust your judgment. Now I can read it and next time I call, we can discuss it."

Despite this errand having gone totally awry, despite that all her intentions were just forced into reverse, an imminent book talk produced a *ping!* inside Cassidy. Just like—

"Just like back at college," he said.

Right. Just like that.

He bent and picked a different book off the floor by his feet. "I grabbed this, too." He offered it to her.

It was the book he'd mentioned reading himself last night. She flipped through it at first to be polite, but a sentence caught her eye. She read the paragraph, then the page, and turned it.

She'd read another page before remembering herself. She snapped her head up. Eric was watching her with a half-smile that was so simply sexy, she nearly dropped the heavy book. She shrugged a tiny shrug of embarrassment. "Sorry, I found an interesting part."

"The whole book is absorbing." He took it back. "You'll find out because I'm getting it for you. Let's go."

His long legs carried him out the aisle quickly. Cassidy jogged a few steps to catch up. "Don't," she said, tugging his sleeve.

"It's a present. Just say 'thank you.'"

"Why?"

"Because it's polite." The shop owner raised his eyebrows at Cassidy, curious. She was always alone before.

She rolled her eyes and he grinned, bagging the two books. She was glad he wasn't annoyed at them for making noise in the silent store.

Eric signed the credit card slip.

"Why?" she repeated.

"See you," he said to the shop owner. Eric held the door open for Cassidy, then followed her through it. "It's a thank-you gift," he said, pausing on the last step to button his trench coat. From the bottom up, Cassidy noticed. Same as always.

"For what?"

"For not having me thrown out of the embassy when you found out I took an advisory job."

Cassidy pulled her gloves on. "Ambassador Cole wanted you there."

"So?"

"So, I doubt he'd have you thrown out because I was pissy."

"I don't know about that," Eric said as they started to walk. "He certainly thinks the world of you, with good reason. I'm sure he'd prefer you to be happy."

Cassidy pretended her palms were two sides of a scale and alternated tipping each side up and down. "Cassidy's feelings, world peace. Hmm. Tough choice."

"He could have gotten someone else just as good. But you tolerated me, and now I get to work on this possibly historic plan. It means a lot to me. More than the price of a book. But it's the least I can do." Halfway down the block, he stopped at a pub. He held open the door, told the hostess, "Two," and led Cassidy halfway to a table in a deserted corner before she realized what was happening.

"What? No, no," she protested. "I have to go home."

"Let's eat first."

She shook her head.

"It's dinnertime. You have to eat. I have to eat. We're together at the moment. Just eat. Come on."

She sat with a defiant thud on the wooden chair, which made her back teeth bash together.

"Ow, I saw that," Eric said, clearly trying not to laugh.

She slowly and deliberately crossed her eyes.

"A-ah," he said, holding out his palm to shield the view. "I hate that, it's disgusting." As if she didn't know that.

She waited until he tentatively dropped his hand and peered at her. Then she did it again. He grabbed a handful of sugar packets off the table and threw them at her. She laughed, really hard. When the waitress came by, they had to wave her away until Cassidy could contain herself long enough to order in a civilized manner.

"The ambassador should see you now," Eric said. "I bet he'd reconsider your responsibilities."

She nodded in agreement.

"How did you get that job, anyway?"

"Worked my way up."

"No, I mean, how did you get into the embassy in the first place?"

"I…found out about it, and got it," she said, and it was the weird truth. A few weeks after the graduation she hadn't attended, she'd arrived home from her waitressing job—home to her one-room apartment in a seedy area of a town near Saunders—to find a message on her answering machine. A woman who didn't leave her name, but knew Cassidy's, and who left details about the plum London job and a phone number. Cassidy had gone for an interview with a "recruiter," but the waiting room had been suspiciously empty of hopeful college grads. One day later she got a call accepting her, and she'd left for London forever the following week. She'd always been convinced she'd been somehow handpicked, that the interview was a staged formality, but the job was certainly real, and incredible—the kind of job she'd worked for her whole life. The kind of job she thought she didn't deserve anymore after she'd…really messed up.

"What kinds of things do you do?" he asked. "Besides what I've seen."

She described her various duties, which eventually led into a broader political discussion of world affairs. Although they couldn't talk about the details of the initiative in such a public place, they discussed past British-American diplomacy and recent news developments, and debated some comments made on TV talk shows. Cassidy felt another thrill surge through her to be able to do this again. To match her brain up to his and really think, really get to the essence of world events, to hear his opinions and challenge them or share them, and to show off a little of her own knowledge. To pick up where they had left off.

It had been so long. And he was so close. She could smell his skin and it was as though the home she'd left behind had come to be with her again. Home and warmth and love.

When their tea arrived, Eric said, "You know, I've long been a distant admirer of Ambassador Cole. But now I'm getting insight into the brilliant and very compassionate man that he is."

"I'm amazed every day that I work with him," Cassidy answered, blowing on her tea before sipping it.

Eric waited a beat. "That's funny. It was on a far less grand scale, of course, but I distinctly recall you once saying that about Gilbert Harrison. You admired his intelligence and the way he cared about every student. He was a bit of a hero to you."

Cassidy acknowledged his assessment with a half nod, staring into her teacup. Gilbert certainly had been a man she admired, a man who could do no wrong—until that day in his office when she accidentally discovered he was as infallible as anyone. She had never said anything to him, and he had never offered her an explanation, but their relationship had quietly deteriorated. Perhaps she'd been too young to know how to be a real friend then, but now, he needed all the friends he could get.

"I'll write that letter on his behalf right away," she said. "I promise."

She waited for an argument, for another entreaty to come home, but it didn't happen. Eric merely nodded, changed the subject by mentioning a health-care controversy back in the United States, and their spirited conversation resumed, lasting until after three tea refills.

"Well, it's probably time for you to go," Eric finally

said, and Cassidy realized that for the first time since he'd arrived, she wasn't the one to point that out. They settled their bill and left the restaurant. Cassidy turned up her collar as Eric put two fingers in his mouth and impressively whistled for a cab.

"No," Cassidy protested as Eric opened the cab door for her.

"Well, the cab's certainly not for me. My hotel is just across the street."

She looked across the street and all she could think was, That's where Eric's staying. That's where Eric's sleeping. That's where Eric showers…

Eric would leave for Boston again soon. And after that, she would look at that hotel every day on the way home from work and think, That's where Eric stayed. That's where he slept…

He was a part of her life, now, again.

She saw him give the cabbie money, and she opened her mouth but Eric put one finger over her lips. "I want you to get home safely. Don't argue."

Her lips were parted. She wanted to close her mouth, but that would have meant dragging her lips along his bare finger to do so. She tried not to breathe, and he took his hand away.

Her heart pounded in her ears. She tossed her briefcase into the back seat, then slid in next to it. Eric leaned in and handed her the book he'd bought her.

"Nice skirt, by the way," he said, and slammed the door.

The cab glided away from the curb. The seat was velvety and warm, but the floor was sticky. She gave the driver the address and twisted in her seat to see out the back window. It was fogged over, but she could just barely make out a dark figure jogging across the street and hopping up the curb on the other side.

The phone was ringing when she unlocked the front door. Her home phone. She knew who it was. She fell onto the sofa and picked it up without saying hello.

Eric didn't say anything, either. They sat in each other's silence.

"I take it you made it home," Eric said after a long while.

"Mmm-hmm."

"Good.

"Lunch tomorrow?" he inquired.

She hesitated, but for far less time than she had in the last week or so. "Mmm-hmm."

Cassidy remembered long nights at the Saunders library, both pretending to study textbooks when they were really studying each other. He'd always called her when they each went home, because he wanted to say good-night. She'd always pointed out he'd already said good-night, but he'd always said he wanted to do it as close to her bedtime as possible. The word bed was a thick word back then, full of promise for the future.

"Well," he said. "Good night."

His voice in her ear simultaneously excited her body and soothed her heart.

"Good...good night," she said back.

She waited until he hung up. She replaced the phone on the cradle. Then she switched off the light and lay her head on the arm of the sofa. Her intention was to ruminate on their conversation, on the way his smile deepened new lines in the corners of his eyes, but within seconds, she was fast asleep.

"Big mistake, Miss Maxwell. Big, big mistake."

Cassidy swallowed, and it was so hard to do that she actually had to push on her throat with both hands to unblock it.

"But," he said, "I think you know that."

Randall Greene approached her desk with long, scary strides. She couldn't back up, she couldn't move. He put his elbows on the desk, leaning close into her face. "Dean's list every semester, for almost four years," he said. His breath, a sickening combination of corn chips and coffee, blew into her nose. His words echoed against the sides of her skull. "Such a smart girl. How did you get into this?"

I don't know. I know I screwed up. It was just this one time. I was so behind. Please…

"And more importantly, how in the world are you going to get out of this?"

I don't know, I don't know, I don't know…

"This will ruin you. Straight-A Cassidy Maxwell. Flunking. And the administration doesn't take kindly to this kind of thing, you know. So unkindly, in fact, that they just might throw you out for good. No degree. After all that work."

She tried hard not to whimper but she heard the desperate, high-pitched sound come out of her anyway.

"But don't look so glum, chum," he said, glancing out the small window on the door before putting a large hand on her shoulder. He leaned into it, into her, pushing her down in the seat. Her knees cracked. "You do have one option. An option I'm not willing to offer very often. But you—you're one of my special students."

He lifted a finger and twirled a lock of her hair around it. Then he yanked down, pulling a sharp pain from her scalp. Tears that had already been close saturated her bottom lashes.

"We all make mistakes," he said, nodding with his chin to the term paper on her desk. "But you don't have to live with this one. Why should you? It will ruin everything..."

He bent even closer, removed his glasses, locked his hard eyes onto hers and whispered his solution into her face...

Cassidy woke up and tumbled weakly from the sofa onto the floor. She crawled on her hands and knees toward the bathroom, rising shakily to her feet when she reached the door. Without flipping on the light, she turned on the water and splashed her face. She looked at herself in the mirror, a pale outline in the dark, drops dribbling down her forearms.

She would have given anything to have nightmares. Nightmares were mind tricks, illusions. Nightmares weren't real.

No, Cassidy didn't have nightmares. She had real-life memories, in full color, in intricate detail.

She hadn't had this one come to her in the middle of the night in quite a while. The intensity of it hit her again, and she sat on the bathroom floor.

This had no doubt been a warning from her conscience, a warning about Eric. She had gone to bed feeling about him…well, almost the way she used to.

But there was no way in hell she could get that close to him again. Because to get as close to him as she'd been earlier in her life, she'd have to be completely honest with him. Tell him all her truths.

Even after all this time, Cassidy knew she could not bear the disapproval, the rejection, that would certainly follow such a confession.

She was dangerously close to being in a position for that rejection. There was no point in reprimanding herself for falling for Eric's charms. What she needed to do was to fix things before they got out of hand. Out of her hands.

Chapter Seven

Cassidy drummed her fingers on her desk and checked her little black clock: 12:35. She drummed some more. She looked again: 12:37.

A couple of advisers wandered into the front office, and Cassidy sprang into action. She shrugged into her red jacket and grabbed her coat off the brass rack in the corner. She exited her office just as Eric was striding toward it.

He smiled at her. She felt like a mean, terrible person.

But she quickly remembered how terrible she would seem if she were to ever tell him the truth.

"Eric," she said, as if surprised to see him. "I'm sorry, but I have to back out of lunch. I have an appointment I forgot about."

"With who?" he asked.

Any other person in her office would have just assumed the appointment was important and accepted the sparse explanation. She should have known Eric would press for details.

Sophie walked past them. "Ah, Sophie," Cassidy said to Eric.

Sophie turned. "Yes?"

Yikes. "Are…are you all set?" Cassidy asked.

Sophie wrinkled her forehead. "I made those calls and was about to e-mail you…"

"Fine, grab your coat and we'll talk about it over lunch."

"Lunch?"

"Don't tell me you forgot," Cassidy said, willing the young woman to play along.

Sophie darted the briefest glance at Eric and said, "No, of course not. Let me get my things."

"I'll come with you," Cassidy said, but Eric took her elbow.

"You're running out on me," he said.

She stared into his face, that handsome, hurt, disappointed face, and found herself unable to do it for long.

Would she have to be a mean person for the rest of her life?

"I've got to go," she mumbled, and dashed to Sophie's desk, where the junior aide was zipping her jacket. They left the front office together and Cassidy refused to turn around. She couldn't look at him there alone.

* * *

A half hour later the two women were waiting for their entrées at a nearby restaurant. Despite the crowded lunch hour, they were lucky enough to get a table at the large picture window overlooking Hyde Park. They hadn't really spoken, except to express delight at the good seating.

Sophie Messing was in her mid-twenties, with bold brown hair chopped in pin-straight layers around her face. Her eyes were bright bits of blue and very large, giving her a permanent appearance of having just become wide-awake. Her personality was wide-awake, too. In the office, she was up for any task. Even her most mundane jobs were done with flair and a grin. Perhaps other bosses would have viewed it as young, green eagerness, but Cassidy had sensed the exuberance would be just as strong when Sophie reached retirement age.

She was the antithesis to Cassidy herself.

Both women sipped diet Coke through striped bendy straws. Sophie eventually spoke. "You know, I was surprised you asked me to lunch. Even if I was a bit of an excuse to get away from that man Eric Barnes." She grinned. "I'm glad. It's nice to get a chance to get to know you outside the office. Except for embassy functions, none of us in the office ever see you. Some people think—" Sophie cut herself off and reddened, biting her lower lip.

Cassidy was startled. She'd never thought anyone thought anything about her, except as someone they worked with. The idea that they speculated about her was unsettling. What could they be saying? That she was distant, snotty, had a superiority complex?

"What do they think?" she forced herself to ask, very quietly.

Sophie looked into her boss's eyes. "Some people, including me, I admit, wondered if you're, maybe... lonely."

Cassidy hadn't expected that assessment at all. Something in her expression caused Sophie's rush to continue. "You're a great boss, considerate of us, always acknowledge when we do a good job or stay late. You bring us treats. You seem like such a sweet person. I haven't been here long but even people that have been here a few years have commented that you're so private. No one knows for sure even if you're married, or where you grew up."

Cassidy took a breath, opened her mouth and closed it again.

"Anyway," Sophie said, "I'm being presumptuous. Maybe you're a real social butterfly and it's just not with coworkers—"

"I'm not," Cassidy said flatly, and had to laugh when Sophie did.

Their salads arrived and they asked each other get-to-know-you questions. Sophie had grown up and gone to college in Connecticut, and currently was in a long-distance relationship with her fiancé, who was planning to move to London in six months. Cassidy revealed being from New Jersey but guarded her association with Eric Barnes. Though Sophie preferred fiction to history books, they found they both loved Frank Sinatra songs and Nicolas Cage movies, and both considered themselves experts at blackjack.

When their check arrived, Cassidy was sorry they had to go back to work. It had been many years since she'd enjoyed the company of another woman. She grabbed the check and insisted on paying it. "Please," she said as Sophie protested. "Lunch was my idea anyway."

"It will be my idea next time," Sophie assured her.

It was such a nice, assuming thing to say.

"This was fun. Listen, Cassidy," Sophie added. "At work, you're always my boss. But on the outside, well, you don't have to be my friend. But I think I would like to be able to say I'm your friend."

Cassidy clutched her wallet as she heard the kind words. "Me, too," she said quietly.

The waiter took the check and Cassidy's credit card. "Thanks," she said to Sophie.

Her new friend snorted. "For what?"

"You...you saved me today."

"I figured as much," Sophie said as the waiter brought back the check with a pen. "But I'm dying to know why. Maybe soon, you can fill me in." She winked.

The phone rang on the other end of the line and Eric couldn't stop the surge that ran through him at the thought of her voice.

She'd bolted on him earlier today, and it had stung, but he was now living and working on another continent because of her. He couldn't stand to let her off so easy.

Plus, they'd had a great talk last night, and the night before. So there was no sin in trying to strike up another one. Besides, it was possible she was regretting pushing him away, and he knew her stubbornness would never let her admit that, so it was best he made the move.

Eric was sitting at the large desk in his hotel room. He hadn't even changed out of his suit. He'd just grabbed dinner, come back and picked up the phone. The dinner was sitting in a leaky bag on the blotter in front of him, having been relegated to less of a priority than talking to Cassidy.

The phone stopped ringing. She had picked it up. But she was refusing to initiate the conversation with a hello.

She had done this last time, but this time he distinctly felt a hostile vibe on the wire. He decided to say nothing, also.

Several minutes went by with nothing but steady breathing. "I know it's you, Eric," she finally said, and he could hear from her compressed voice that her back teeth were jammed together.

"Good," he said. "Greetings unnecessary. I like that. We can just jump into good stuff. I'm reading this book, and—"

"It's not going to work."

"What's not?"

A long silence again. "Whatever you're trying to do."

"Just trying to be your friend again."

"You're trying to make me come home to Saunders to testify at the hearing."

Eric attempted to think of a response that would let

him off the hook without making him admit that she was technically correct.

"And," she added, "you're trying to make me fall in love with you again."

Eric swallowed. Not just at the words, but that they'd come out of Cassidy's mouth. Even back at school, when they were so enamored of each other that the world went blurry around them, she'd shown her affection with smiles and meaningful light touches and flirty glances. He'd known how she'd felt, but she'd never come out and outright said it. That wasn't her style.

Anyway, she was wrong. "You're wrong," he told her. Okay, he needed to bring her back to Massachusetts. And he *was* trying to be her friend, because it seemed unnatural not to. And, if pressed, he'd have to admit he still secretly hoped she'd trust him enough to tell him why she'd run away ten years ago. His foolish pride longed for the long-overdue information. Just for closure.

But he never, ever, ever had the intention of making Cassidy fall in love with him again.

Because he couldn't stand it if she left again.

"You're wrong," he repeated, a little bit louder.

"Really?" she asked, and it was not a request for clarification. It was a challenge for him to deny it again.

Could he?

He remembered the way it had hurt when she'd taken off with her junior staffer for lunch, breaking their plans. It was just a small hurt, a tiny scratch on his soul compared to the deep, gaping gash she'd inflicted once upon a time. But it was an echo of a similar pain.

For the last couple of days all he could think about—when he wasn't working—was how much fun they were having now, the things she'd said in the pub, the things he'd said on the phone, what had made her laugh again.

He'd been encouraging her to open up to him and she was, but in that process, he now realized, he'd been opening himself up, too.

And that wasn't smart. He could not, would not, fall in love with a woman who had broken his heart already. Not just broken it, but ripped it out and flung it into a harsh wind, rendering it impossible for him to ever love anyone else. Or to even come close to love.

"Believe me, Cassidy," he said very quietly. "You've given me every reason to not make you fall in love with me again."

She didn't respond, which was no surprise. His pulse was pounding hard in his temple.

"Let's change the subject," he said with false gaiety.

"Um," Cassidy said. "No. Let's not, um…" Her voice trailed off into nothing.

"So you don't even want to keep up our renewed friendship?"

Please don't say it, he thought. *Don't say it. I don't want to fail me, or Gilbert, for that matter.*

"It's best, I think," she said slowly, "if you don't call me."

Eric didn't have to wait long before he felt that pang in his chest. A little harder than when she'd blown him off for lunch. He'd sworn he could handle himself, but it seemed he was doomed to hurt whenever she was around.

"And, at the office—" she added.

"You won't have to worry about that for long," he said. "I'm going to Belfast."

"Oh." She didn't say anything more. "Right."

"I assume you knew the ambassador is going."

"We had a press conference a couple of hours ago."

"I had actually thought you might go, as well."

"No, I need to stay and handle some things here."

"We're leaving Thursday night."

"I know."

"So I'm sure we could deal with a couple of days of random bumping into each other." He tried to keep his tone light, but his heart felt very heavy. "Maybe when I'm gone, you'll—" He stopped. What was he going to say? *Miss me? Maybe you'll miss me?* No. He did not want to say that.

"I will," she said.

What? "You'll what?"

"I'll write that letter for Gilbert. It will be done when you come back. You'll be leaving after that, right?"

Eric closed his eyes. "Yes."

"Then I'll have it for you."

Eric opened his eyes again and stared at the painting on the wall above the bed pillows. A small yellow boat floated on a serene turquoise lake. The painting was perhaps meant to soothe, to calm a harried hotel guest, but it agitated Eric to think it was a depiction of a place that probably only existed in the artist's imagination. If Eric searched his whole life, he was willing to bet he'd never find that lake or the peace it implied.

"I suppose we've made some progress," he said to Cassidy. "You're running from me again. But at least, this time, I'm getting some verbal confirmation. It's a step up in civility from cowardly standing someone up under a tree. For ten years."

He heard a sharp intake of breath and pretended he didn't care that she was hurting now, too.

He hung up, so he could fool himself into believing he was the one who walked away this time. Then he dropped his face into his folded arms on the desk. He stayed that way a long time. He never ate his dinner.

Eric crossed paths with Cassidy just a few times over the next two days, and each occasion was uneventful. He saw Cassidy and Sophie returning from lunch twice, laughing and chatting, though Cassidy's smile dropped off her face each time she spied Eric. She avoided meeting his eye every time. There were also times he saw her without her knowledge. He watched her stride to the copy machine several times, moving as easily and gracefully in neck-breakingly high heels as he used to see her move in beat-up sneakers. He saw her lean over a cubicle to speak to someone, her dark green trousers stretching over her perfect rear.

Both mornings, he'd awakened after dreams of her kisses that had made him thrash around and tear blankets from the corners of the bed in unconscious frustration.

Part of him wanted to go home and to never speak to

her again. Part of him wanted to corner her and to make her tell him that she tossed and turned at night, also. Part of him wanted to kiss her, to feel her surrender her stubbornness and admit she'd wasted a decade they could have been together.

Packing a bag in his hotel room Thursday, he decided to take all those parts and put them together to focus on his important job. Beating himself up was useless. Technically he was in the same exact position he was when he'd first flown here, with Cassidy not speaking to him and still having no idea why she'd fled Saunders.

Well, he wasn't quite where he'd started. He had one more kiss to add to his dusty collection of mind pictures.

All this woman did was wreck him. Maybe he had done himself a favor by coming here. Maybe he had to see her again and get to know her again to prove to himself that she wouldn't have been right for him. That it wouldn't have worked.

Yes, he thought, hefting up his suitcase and leaving the room. He came to London. He did what he had to do. Now it was time to do what he had to do for the rest of the world.

Then he could just go home.

Cassidy had long ago reconciled herself to the fact that while on Friday evenings most single young women were dressing up to hit the town, she herself stayed home and watched the news over dinner for one. It was usually okay.

As she settled herself on her sofa with a generous helping of baked macaroni and cheese, she wondered if, had they not had their last conversation, she would have been going somewhere with Eric tonight.

In the time since she'd left America, how many single young women had had the pleasure of dressing up, knowing they were going to meet the sexy Eric Barnes?

No. No. She would not engage in this self-torture. It had distracted her enough in the past couple of days, and would surely continue when he left for Boston soon. She forced herself to relax. She needed a mental rest.

She thought about calling Sophie, who unwittingly was the bright spot in Cassidy's past forty-eight hours. They'd gone for lunch twice more, and both lunches had gone long because their conversations were so fun. Cassidy had forgotten what it was like to have a female pal, and was grateful she had one now, because she'd need it after casting aside her oldest best friend.

Again.

She turned on the TV with the remote. At least she had gotten home at a more reasonable hour than she had been lately. After sending the ambassador and his advisers off to Belfast, she'd only had a few things left to do. She had to go in this weekend, so she'd kicked herself out early tonight.

When the breaking news hit, Cassidy's first stupid thought was that even now she still wasn't accustomed to hearing bad news in a British accent. Everything sounded lovely in that accent, even news of horrific car bombs that—

Car bombs that—

Oh, God.

Cassidy dropped her fork and turned it up. Words smashed into her brain.

Car bomb. Belfast. U.S. ambassador to London.

Blast. Panic.

Motorcade en route to talks on proposed peace initiative…too early to know what happened…not enough information at this time…sources say several injured… unknown who may have been—

The live picture at the scene showed only heavy smoke and flames toasting the shells of several cars.

Cassidy realized she was clutching herself, her arms tight around her midsection. She was rocking, whimpering.

The ambassador.

Eric, Eric, Eric, Eric…

She dropped her bowl on the floor, ran to her briefcase, yanked out her phone. She shook so hard, she had to hold her wrist steady with her other hand to read the electronic display.

No messages.

She walked as if in a daze back to the sofa and flipped through channels. The incident was all over the local news, London panicking about much-loved Ambassador Cole.

Her cell phone rang and she nearly threw it across the room in fright. She pressed a button. "Hello?" she cried.

"Cassidy, it's Sophie. Did you hear?"

"Just saw…on TV…"

"Well, if you don't know anything else, then that's all anyone knows. Do you need me to come in to the office?"

"I'm at home."

"Okay, well, are you going in? Will you need help? I can be there in fifteen. I was supposed to go to see my fiancé tomorrow for a few days but I'll just exchange the plane ticket."

There was nothing she could do at the office but wait anyway, the logical part of her knew. "N-no."

"Cassidy, are you all right? It will be all right. I'm sure the ambassador is just fine. He probably just hasn't gotten a chance to call you yet, I mean, it just happened..."

Sophie's words faded in and out of Cassidy's comprehension. "Eric," she whispered.

"Did you say 'Eric'?" Sophie asked, and then there was a short pause. "Oh, oh, okay. Cassidy, I'm coming over."

"No—"

"I'm coming to your flat. Right now. Give me the address."

Cassidy recited it, too numb to protest.

"I'll be there in a few minutes. It's okay, honey. It's okay. Take it easy. I'll be there soon."

Cassidy let Sophie in and the young woman hugged her. Taken by surprise, Cassidy hugged her back, burying her face in Sophie's soft blue sweater.

"Everything's going to be okay," Sophie murmured.

She had never told Sophie who Eric was, and what was between them, but it was clear her new friend had a keen woman's intuition.

Sophie smoothed a hand over Cassidy's hair, then dropped a bag from the market on the table. She unpacked hot chocolate mix, cookies and soup. Cassidy wandered back to the sofa and kept an eye on the television. Nothing yet, but it had only been about a half hour. Sophie looked at her from the kitchen, then came back into the room with a sponge. She picked up the bowl and cleaned the floor.

"Don't," Cassidy said.

"It's okay, just sit tight."

Cassidy stared at the TV without seeing much. They repeated the information she already knew about four hundred and fifty times. At a commercial, she heard her teakettle whistle, and Sophie came in with two steaming mugs.

"I know tea is the thing in this part of the world," she confessed, "but I far prefer hot chocolate."

Cassidy tried to smile, but couldn't. "Thank you."

"No problem. I like your flat."

Cassidy surveyed her living room. She had always liked it, too. Now she wondered if it was the place she'd have to remember for eternity as where she was when she'd heard Eric was—

Her eyes filled with tears.

Sophie wisely didn't ask any questions or give reassurances she couldn't really give. She just sat with Cassidy for what seemed forever. After about twenty minutes, Cassidy's phone jingled in her lap. She grabbed it and Sophie put a hand on her arm.

"Cassidy?" Ambassador Cole called over static. "Can you hear me?"

"Yes, yes, Ambassador," Cassidy shouted, not knowing if he could hear her.

"I'm all right," he said. "Everyone's—" She lost his sentence in a crackle.

"I can't hear you," she said, but suddenly the static ceased.

"That's better," he said to her. "We're all okay."

"Eric?" she asked.

"Yes, I said everyone's—" He cut his sentence short and this time it wasn't the fault of static. "Eric Barnes is fine," he said slowly. "I just saw him a couple of minutes ago."

"Oh, thank God," Cassidy said. *Thank you, thank you, thank you.*

"Thank God," Sophie echoed, interpreting the good news from Cassidy's side of the conversation.

"Yes," Ambassador Cole said. "I'm sorry I didn't get a chance to call right away. It was hectic, to say the very least."

"What happened? TV news still has no idea."

"A bomb went off in a parked car on the route our motorcade was traveling. All of us are fine, but some innocent bystanders got hurt, I'm very sorry to say."

"That's awful."

"Yes. But the talks will still go on tomorrow as planned. I've stepped up security there at the embassy, so I want you to work from home this weekend, all right? And be sure everyone in the front office does the same."

"Don't you want me to meet the plane tomorrow?"

"No need. I'm on a different schedule now, so I'm

not sure what time I'll be there. I'll check in, and I'll see you Monday. I'll talk to everyone else then."

"Sure. I'm so relieved you're all right, Ambassador. I was…scared."

"Everything's fine," he said, with authority in his tone. "And, Cassidy?"

"Yes?"

"Would you like me to ask Eric to call you?"

Cassidy felt her face heat up. "Um, no. No need. Don't even bother to tell him I was—"

"Sure," he promised.

She hung up. "Everyone's okay," she said to Sophie.

"I guessed as much. I'm so happy."

Cassidy sat back and unclenched her fists and her teeth, letting the tension ease from her body.

Sophie jumped up and retrieved the box of cookies from the kitchen. She ripped open the package and handed Cassidy a few before stuffing one into her own mouth. "Celebration food," she said around a mouthful of crumbs. "I'm trying to decide if I should ask you about Eric."

Cassidy crunched on her cookie, not surprised. Tonight she'd made herself pretty obvious. Even the ambassador was starting to get a clue about her private life.

"Is he your boyfriend? Tell me to shut up, and I won't ask anything. But this was obviously hard for you."

Cassidy nodded and picked up another cookie. "He's not my boyfriend. He was—"

"He was your boyfriend?"

"He was…something," Cassidy answered truthfully.

"You got away from him pretty quickly the other day. I think he has feelings for you."

Cassidy raised an eyebrow.

"He does," Sophie insisted. "He's been watching you the last couple of days."

"He has not," Cassidy said, knowing her friend was right.

"And you have feelings for him."

It would have been useless for Cassidy to contradict that.

"I don't want to talk about it anymore," Cassidy said.

"Okay, I'm sorry."

"It's not you," Cassidy said. "I…never talk about it."

"Secrets," Sophie said, and shook her head sadly. "I know what that's like."

"What?"

"When you have something you can't talk about. It's hard, carrying it around all the time."

Sophie? What could wide-open, cheerful Sophie be carrying?

"But this weekend," Sophie said, "I'm going to do something about it. I've just made the decision."

"To do what?" Cassidy asked.

"Oh, you know, I shouldn't even be talking about this. I came over to help you."

"You did," Cassidy pointed out. "My crisis is over. If you have a crisis, let me return the favor."

Sophie smiled, but it was the saddest smile Cassidy

had ever seen on her. "I'm really the only one who can help me."

Cassidy didn't respond. She waited for Sophie to continue.

"Ken's the best thing that ever happened to me," Sophie said. "He's wonderful. He's sexy. He's perfect. But…I'm not perfect. I did something—once. I made a big mistake."

Cassidy was surprised, but kept her face neutral. Sophie didn't elaborate on her sin, but Cassidy, with her own hidden past, didn't expect her to.

"When Ken asked me to marry him, it was like the sun came out on my whole life, you know?" Sophie said. "He's amazing. But if he ever found out what I— This is something he would be extremely unhappy about. If he finds out, I could lose him."

"How could he find out?"

"Truthfully, the only way he'd find this out is if I told him."

"Then what—"

"I'm going to tell him."

"What?" Cassidy couldn't mask her incredulity. "What? Why?" *Don't tell him,* she thought. *You can't. There are some secrets you don't talk about, some secrets you have to keep forever…*

"In six months he's going to move to a different country, to live here and marry me. He's turning his world upside-down for me. I owe him the truth."

Cassidy shook her head. "Don't be angry with me for saying so, but you're making a mistake."

Sophie gave her sad smile again. "I appreciate your honesty, but I disagree. I've thought about this a long time. I might lose him, but the real mistake is to not tell him. How can I pledge my life to this man, make vows, while keeping something inside that he's completely ignorant of? Then our whole marriage would be a lie."

"But you said he'd never know."

"But *I* would. See, if he leaves me, my heart will be broken. But if I don't tell him the truth, if I live day after day with him without giving him a chance to learn the real me, that will hurt much deeper for far longer."

"Oh, please, Sophie, don't." Cassidy grabbed her hand. "Please, I'm begging you."

"Why?" Sophie asked, confusion spreading across her face.

"I just couldn't stand to—" *have him reject me* "—see you get rejected, when it doesn't have to be that way."

"That was my opinion for a long time," Sophie said, "but it's just too hard to hold this all inside."

"It gets easier with time," Cassidy said, but she knew that wasn't true.

Sophie shook her head. "No."

"You're brave," Cassidy said. *Far braver than me, and it will hurt you.*

"Not really. Even though I made this big decision to do the right thing, I still can't bring myself to tell him to his face. I told him I'm arriving Sunday. So I'm going to write him a letter on the plane trip tomorrow. I'll leave it at his apartment and stay at my mother's.

Then—I'll see what happens next." She sighed and stretched her arms over her head, studying Cassidy's worried face.

"I know you think I'm being foolish, but I know I'm not," Sophie insisted again. "Besides, every situation is different. This is right for me, even if you think it isn't right for you."

Cassidy was taken aback. "What—how do you—"

"Oh, I'm not psychic or anything," Sophie said. "I don't know what your story is. But by the way you just reacted to my decision, I'm guessing that you have a secret, too."

Cassidy said nothing.

"I've done a lot of thinking. It's all about trust," Sophie said.

"What is?"

"Everything. When you trust people, it gives them the fullest opportunity to understand you. And care about you." She paused to let her young wisdom sink in, then added, "Of course, this all might be very premature, stupid advice, but I'll know soon enough, right? I'll be back Wednesday. I may very well need you to come over and bring *me* hot chocolate," she joked weakly.

"Or help you pick your bridal gown," Cassidy said with more conviction than she felt. "Are you really sure about this?"

"Yes," Sophie said. "In fact, it will be a relief to get it out. Even if it doesn't have good consequences. I can take the consequences and then it will be over, either way. It will be better than what I've been doing. I'm sure."

Sophie stayed for a little while longer, watching TV and chatting, and before she left, they hugged again, initiated by Cassidy this time. "If you change your mind, it's okay," Cassidy said.

"I won't," Sophie said. "I just have to do this." She put on her coat.

As Cassidy waved goodbye to Sophie, she worried for her. And for Ken. And for Eric.

And for herself.

Because as soon as she'd hung up with the ambassador, as soon as she'd discovered that Eric was safe, she had made her own decision about something she had to do.

Chapter Eight

Sitting in the back of the chauffeured car, looking out at the after-midnight rain, Eric wearily leaned his forehead on the cold window.

Returning to London shouldn't exactly feel like coming home, but after yesterday, he was relieved to be anywhere with even the smallest degree of familiarity.

Yesterday in Belfast, in the back of a car much like this one, he had been chatting with other members of the U.S. peace delegation on the way to the talks, thoughts of the initiative competing in his head with thoughts of Cassidy. He hadn't been prepared for the noise, a deafening blast of shattering glass. He instinctively covered his face. His ears rang, and someone pushed a hand on the back of his neck, pushing him to the carpet, yelling at him to stay down. The car had stopped short and Eric had tasted blood on his bottom lip where he'd accidentally chomped down.

Cassidy, he remembered thinking and possibly saying out loud in the panicked car.

Then he was being helped from the car, guided to safety with his confused but unhurt colleagues. Parked cars were burning. When they were escorted to a safe place indoors, everyone talked at once.

After Ambassador Cole's adamant insistence, the peace talks had gone on, a little later than scheduled. They had continued this morning and lasted much of the day before the ambassador and his weary staff returned to London. Weary from a scare, but also weary from productive sessions with leaders from the Northern Ireland factions.

Eric was deposited at the same hotel he'd left, where he'd requested the same room. Once again, the feeling of some familiarity was welcome.

It seemed the moment he'd stepped on the curb that the rain intensified, and he dashed to the door, stepping in an ankle-deep puddle on the way. He paused under the awning to shake his foot and stepped into the lobby.

It was not an ornate hotel, more functional than beautiful. At this hour on a Sunday morning, it was silent, with the older guests having gone to bed hours ago and the younger guests not back from the pubs yet.

The man at the desk recognized Eric and gave him back his key. Eric turned to head for the elevator, but stopped short at the sight of Cassidy sleeping on the lobby sofa.

She was curled up in a corner, one hand under her head, the other holding her coat lapels closed. Her hands had relaxed in sleep, though, and one lapel had drooped down to reveal a couple of inches of a rose-colored thermal top. Her auburn hair draped over the sofa arm. She was wearing jeans, and Eric realized that though she'd once been the girl who wore jeans every day, he hadn't seen her wear them the whole time he'd been here. Her lips were open just the slightest fraction of an inch.

She was there for him.

He wondered how long she'd been here. The cab driver had said that it rained all day in London, but her red umbrella on the floor was dry. Her hair was dry, also, but the moisture had fluffed out its normally sleek strands.

He wondered why she hadn't been asked to leave. He turned to ask the desk clerk. The young man was looking at Cassidy with a soft expression that made it crystal clear to Eric why she had been allowed to stay.

The clerk realized he'd been noticed, and arranged himself into a more professional demeanor. "I'm sorry, Mr. Barnes, I didn't know she was waiting for you. She was here when I started at midnight."

Eric moved to the sofa and crouched on the floor beside her. She didn't stir. He lifted his hand to rouse her but paused for a second with his hand in the air, unsure of the appropriate place to touch her.

He dropped his hand. "Cassidy," he said in a voice just above a whisper.

She awoke immediately. She didn't quietly rustle

herself from slumber with little ladylike stretches and sighs. No, her eyes popped wide open and, completely unstartled, she stared into Eric's face, penetrating his eyes with her own amber ones. After perhaps a full minute, she sat up with ease, as if her muscles hadn't been cramped from her pretzel position. She climbed down from the sofa and kneeled in front of him so they were face-to-face.

Then she wrapped her arms around his shoulders.

She pressed her face into his neck. Long strands of her hair slid into his mouth. Her fingers curled into his coat. And even through that coat, and her coat, and all that they had on underneath, he could feel her heart banging, pounding hard against his chest.

He dropped his bag on the floor and put his arms around her slight body, pressing her just that much harder against him. He laid his head on her shoulder and rubbed one palm up her back until he was cradling the back of her head. She let out a breath, as if she had been holding it since he'd left, since their last phone call, since she'd seen the news reports. He let out his breath, too, for he'd been holding it for just as long.

Now he felt as though he had come home.

Eric tossed his bag on one of the two double beds as Cassidy sat on the other one and surveyed the room. He found himself hoping she would like it, as if it was a place he'd decorated himself and inhabited full time.

Cassidy bounced very gently on the edge of the bed. Eric wasn't quite sure what she was doing here. After they'd untangled themselves in the lobby, she'd wordlessly headed for the elevator. She'd stood in front of the closed door, waiting for him to press the floor. He'd pressed four and as they waited, he watched her watch him. She darted glances at him, one, two, three, flicking her gaze away every time before he could catch her eyes with his. When the elevator opened, she'd stepped in first, and also stepped out of it first when they reached his floor. She'd followed him to his room and waited as he unlocked it. Now she was sitting on a bed.

One small lamp was on, casting a golden light into her hair.

"It's too late for you to go home," Eric said, as if he was trying to convince her to stay, as if she hadn't made the decision already.

She nodded. "And..." she said.

"And what?" He held his breath.

She closed her eyes and swayed a little. "I'm tired."

Eric carried his toothbrush into the bathroom, snapped on the light and regarded his own face in the mirror. His eyes were red-rimmed from lack of sleep due to the bomb scare and his nearly endless work on the ambassador's initiative. His hair was limp. He rubbed his jawline. His face was scratchy and creased in confusion.

What was going on? It was clear Cassidy wanted to stay here, and he was pretty sure it was because she'd heard of his brush with danger, but he didn't know what her expectations were. And he was afraid of not caring about what her expectations were—and giving in to his urge to push her down on the bed and crawl up her body, removing clothing until her naked, freckled skin was pressed against him…

He realized he'd been staring at himself for a long time. He brushed his teeth, hard and methodically, and after rinsing, his mouth felt clean and worthy of saying what he had to say.

"Cassidy," he called softly through the bathroom door. "I don't know what you're doing here. And in a way, I don't care what you're doing here, only that you're here. Maybe I should demand answers from you. Maybe I should insist you leave and call you a cab. But then, maybe our entire relationship existed just to bring us to this night. I don't know. It's very possible I shouldn't feel this way, but all I want to do right now is go to you and do anything that you need me to do, anything, regardless of what it means for me in the long term. I've waited a long time to see you again, long enough to swallow my pride and accept anything you're willing to give me. Because you're here now.

"So," he added, swallowing hard, "I'm coming out."

His heart beating hard in anticipation, he stepped out into the room, and looked at Cassidy.

She was on her back on the bedspread, her knees still bent over the edge. She'd fallen back and fallen fast asleep.

Eric sat on the opposite bed, feeling the well-used mattress yield a bit under his weight. He considered waking Cassidy, but a moment ago he had promised to give her whatever it was she wanted. Just because she hadn't been awake to hear his speech, didn't mean he wouldn't follow through on it.

Clearly what she wanted was sleep.

It was nearly 3:00 a.m., and the silence in the room was hard to listen to. His body was disturbing that silence, calling out to him, calling out to her to satisfy and satiate.

He got up and went to her. He put his hands under her arms and gently pushed her up the bed until her head reached the pillows. He removed her still wet sneakers, dropping them to the floor. He smiled at her socks, red with little google-eyed black cats. He wondered when she had been in the mood to buy socks like this, and wondered what or who could have put her in that mood. He moved around the bed and lifted her head, sliding a pillow underneath it. Then he pulled up each side of the bedspread, wrapping her up like a burrito.

He took a step back from her bed. He wanted to touch her, to run a finger along her cheek and down her neck and to follow the same trail with his mouth. He wanted to hear her voice in his ear, even if just to cry out his name as he pushed against her and inside her, desperately taking what had been so long denied to him for reasons he still had no clue about.

Her secrets slumbered with her.

He went back to the other bed and lay on his side so that he was facing Cassidy. All the other nights he'd spent in this room, he'd actually slept in the bed where Cassidy was conked out. It was ironic how he'd slid under the blankets of that bed several of those nights—okay, all of those nights—wishing she was there, also.

Now she *was* there and he was over here.

He closed his eyes and passed a hand over them, feeling the grit of sleeplessness. He flicked the wall light switch between the beds, but the dark offered no respite. He took a deep breath, inhaling the hotel air that now contained a hint of flowery perfume. He heard the slight rasp of Cassidy's breathing in the otherwise still room.

Sleep wouldn't come easy to him tonight, but he'd grown accustomed to that since the day he'd arrived in London and kissed Cassidy.

A few hours later Eric realized that he must have gotten some sleep, or else it would be physically impossible to awaken to Cassidy, lying on her side on her bed, her arm under her head, studying him.

He blinked a few times, and she was still there. So it wasn't a dream that she'd spent the night.

What was he thinking? Of course it wasn't a dream. If it had been, she'd be sharing his bed. Naked.

"Good morning," he said, trying to adjust his vision to the daylight that blared in through the window.

In response Cassidy said, "Remember when we camped in your backyard? In your tent?"

It took Eric a moment to realign his brain. He was never very good in the morning. "In my tent…yeah, I believe so. In my backyard…that's right. In the summer. It was brutally hot. Like a real heat wave."

"Terribly hot. And you bought the tent for a trip with

your guy pals and their dads, which I couldn't go on, and so…"

"I suggested you help me try out the tent in the yard one night. To see if it worked." He felt his hair was wild, and tried to smooth it with his hand. "I also remember Mom made us popcorn, that old kind of popcorn, that you held over the stove in a little pan with tin foil? And you had some kind of crazy pink sleeping bag."

"Strawberry Shortcake. Yeah." The corners of her mouth turned up a little. "You fell asleep before me."

"Quite unlike last night."

"Sorry, I was—"

"Tired. I know. You revealed that much before you collapsed. How long did you wait in the lobby?"

"A little while."

"How did you know what time I was coming back?"

"I didn't."

"But you somehow knew to come at two in the morning?"

She shrugged one shoulder.

"Spill it," he said. "How long were you there? Longer than two hours?"

She nodded.

"Longer than four hours?"

"Shut up."

"It was, wasn't it? Longer than six hours?"

She crossed her arms and set her jaw in defiance.

"All right, that answered my question well enough. I interrupted you, I'm sorry. We were in the tent? I fell asleep first?"

She glared at him one more time before backtracking to her memory. "You did. And I listened to your headphones."

"The ones I never let anyone borrow?"

"Ha, ha on you. I used them for at least an hour."

"That was very sneaky."

"That was nothing."

He put his hands behind his head. "Yeah? Enlighten me."

"I kissed you."

A beat went by. Then he sat up, leaning back on his elbows. "No, you didn't."

"I did," she said smugly.

"Why?"

"Because I was nine, and I was curious. And your mouth was right there."

"You kissed me on the mouth?"

She nodded.

He considered a moment. "How was I?"

"Totally icky."

"Thanks a lot.

"Well, I *was* nine."

"I had no idea about any of this." He scratched his shoulder. "Any particular reason you're bringing it up now?"

"Yes."

"What?"

"I have to tell you that, too?"

"I can't make you tell me anything, Cassidy," he pointed out. "We *have* established that by now."

The sheet slipped down his bare skin and he saw Cassidy scan his chest and slightly raise one brow before flicking her gaze back to his face. Eric took a small satisfaction in catching her embarrassment.

"Right," she said, distracted.

"But still, if you felt like telling me, I would like to know why you brought it up."

She rolled over halfway to face the ceiling. "It just seemed like déjà vu. You were asleep."

"And you're thirty and curious? And my mouth is right here?"

He'd meant it as a joke, but she didn't laugh. "Something like that," she said.

He didn't know how to answer that.

"I was scared," she went on.

"Scared—to kiss me?"

"No. I was scared when I saw the bomb on TV. I thought you—" She cut herself off.

Even if Eric had known how to answer, he would have stayed silent. In the last few minutes she'd trusted him with more of her thoughts and feelings than she had since he'd first seen her at the embassy, and he was loath to stop her if she was on a roll.

But she didn't say anything more, apparently finished with her revelations for the time being. Trying not to show his disappointment, Eric fell back onto his pillows and closed his eyes. His body, worn out from emotions, dragged him back toward unconsciousness.

He smelled her before he felt her.

Her skin, the scent of her smooth skin and her hair,

and— He didn't know what it was that caused him to sharply take in a breath. The familiarity that her scent held.

He didn't have much time to consider the nuances before he felt softness on his lips, the sweet pressure of her mouth pressing into his. Her lips were warm on his, and he at first resisted the urge to return it, to deepen it. He forced his lips to stay slack, to make her the instigator, the explorer. His body tightened all over with need, and he fought it as Cassidy ended the kiss then began another one without pulling away. When she did it a third time, he felt the tip of her tongue and couldn't hold back any longer.

He put a hand on the back of her head and gently pushed them even closer together, deepening the contact. She moaned in the back of her throat and he cupped her face with his other hand, spreading his fingers across her skin, caressing with his thumb. She slid her hands up the blankets, then pushed them down to feel his chest, her fingers curling into the hair there.

He refused to open his eyes and meet her gaze, afraid the reminder of who they were would bring her to her senses. Instead he wanted to fill all her senses with pleasure.

She kissed a tantalizing slow trail from the corner of his mouth, down his jaw, to the sensitive skin of his neck. He felt her tasting his skin and he clutched helplessly at her shoulders. Under the blankets, he was only in boxer shorts. He was hers. He would give her anything she desired, right now…

He heard her breathing speed up and grow ragged.

He ran his hands up the sides of her thermal shirt and ran them back down over her front, tentatively at first, but when she gasped, he did it again, with a little more pressure, pausing to flick his thumbs over the tips of her breasts through her cotton shirt.

A knock on the door froze them both. Eric opened his eyes and saw that Cassidy's eyes were wide. They both waited and the second knock sent Cassidy scrambling off him. "Who is it?" he called in a hoarse voice.

"Housekeeping."

"Can you come back later?" he called, and heard the cart wheel away down the hall. He sat up and looked at Cassidy. For one of the first times ever, she was nearly impossible to read. Her face was flushed and he could see her hardened nipples pushing against the fabric of her top. His fingers tingled with having just explored them.

"Are you okay?" he asked, then realized that wasn't very romantic. "Was this—"

Cassidy shook her head in confusion.

"Was that…what you wanted?" he continued, wondering if he could maybe come up with a question that didn't sound so damn stupid.

"I—I don't know."

As much as he wanted her, lusted for her, needed to have her touching him again, he wouldn't push her. "Something's happening here," he said.

She nodded.

"Are you…are you hungry?"

She nodded again.

"Do you want to order breakfast in?"

She looked around the room and so did he, trying to see things as she did. His rumpled bed, his naked chest, even the heat between them was visible. The room was filled to the brim with intimacy, and he thought better of keeping her here, where the intimacy could frighten her away from him for good.

"On second thought let's go out. I trust you can find us a good breakfast spot."

She nodded. "Can I…borrow a shirt or—"

"Of course." He threw off the covers, keeping his back to her, and slid into a pair of jeans. He rummaged through a drawer and pulled out a sweatshirt. "This is really all I have." He tossed it at her.

She let the navy shirt unfold in her lap, staring at the Saunders logo.

Don't go, he silently begged. *I don't know where we're going with things, but I think finally we're going in the right direction. Don't go now.*

She got up and went into the bathroom with her purse. She emerged a few minutes later with the shirt on and a newly done-up ponytail swinging at her neck. He slipped past her, took a fast shower and dressed in jeans and a green T-shirt. When he emerged from the bathroom, she was lying on the bed she'd slept in, flipping cable channels. "No one's claimed responsibility for the bomb," she said.

"Not too surprising. Could have been anyone. There are always some people on both sides of any conflict that don't want to see things resolved peacefully."

"Stupid," she muttered.

"I agree," he said, sitting in the desk chair to put his sneakers on. "Why keep things difficult when you can just move on in a better way?"

She eyeballed him in a way that made it obvious she'd caught his allusion to their personal conflict.

"Cassidy, I—"

"Let's go out," she said. "Everything doesn't have to—be talked about. Can we just…I don't know, feel our way through this?"

Eric thought about his work in the last week. He thought about the way warring sides needed to lay things out, reveal their differences in the open to be able to bring about resolution. If you asked both sides to "feel" their way, conflict would continue. It wasn't really possible to feel the way to compromise.

But this was the most Cassidy had given him so far. She had told him some truths, revealed a bit of her sensual side—so maybe she was right, and he had to let her do things her way so that he could—

What?

Be her boyfriend? The way they'd planned so long ago?

Could that be what he wanted? Was that what was right for him?

He had no idea. Maybe feeling their way *was* best.

"Where are we going?" he asked.

"I told you, I don't know where we're going. Can't we just wait and see if—"

"No, I meant, where are we going for breakfast?"

"Ah." She pressed her lips together, embarrassed.

"Well, on Sunday mornings, I usually get croissants and take a walk to this place that I think you'll—be into."

"Then let's go." He stood and held out his hand. She looked at it for a few long seconds, then put her hand into it and let him lead her from the room.

Eric lumbered along next to Cassidy through Hyde Park feeling as though he was carrying ten extra pounds—a couple from the croissants, the rest from emotion.

"Where are we headed?" he asked.

Cassidy shrugged enigmatically. He could see a huge edifice ahead of them. "What's that?"

"Marble Arch," Cassidy said. "I read it was supposed to be an entranceway for Buckingham Palace but it was too narrow."

"So now it just sort of sits in the middle of traffic," Eric noted. "Guess things don't always work out the way you planned." *But I knew that already,* he thought.

"Here we are," Cassidy said. They stopped in the middle of a little park intersection.

Behind Cassidy, he could see a man standing behind a makeshift podium, ranting against the government's stance on Iraq. He had a few onlookers who alternately cheered and booed. Across the way, a thin woman in thinner clothes gave her own sermon on the impending end of the world. A small group of rebelliously dressed kids watched her, perhaps curious to learn the exact date and time of the apocalypse so they could schedule tattoo sessions appropriately.

"What's going on here?" Eric asked. "Is it some kind of holiday?"

"It's Speaker's Corner," Cassidy said. "Every Sunday, the good people of London traditionally celebrate their right to free speech here."

Eric listened to the snippets of people passionately speaking their piece. "This is wild. You come here every week?"

"I try. I like to hear what people have to say, and I like hearing them say it."

She bent and ran a hand along the pavement, making sure it had dried after last night's downpour, then sat, along the edge, on a patch of grass. Eric sat with her. The air was milder than it had been all week and Cassidy unbuttoned her coat, letting it droop over her shoulders. She lifted her face to the sun rays slicing through the emptying branches. Then she looked at Eric.

Cassidy, beside him in her Saunders shirt, her creamy, makeup-free face in a quiet expression of content.

Those three memories that Eric would never let himself remember? The second one blindsided him, overwhelmed him with its power and insistence.

She had been wearing a shirt like this one, sitting under a tree much like this one, at Saunders. The one they had sat under together countless times. She was a junior, an emerging woman who'd made her mark on campus—and on his heart.

"Cassidy," he said as they watched students hurry to class and to meet friends, scurrying in their daily haste

to get things done. "You know how I feel about you, right?"

She turned to him and, filled with radiant confidence, nodded.

"I want us to be more," he went on, feeling the vibration in his throat as his voice started to tremble.

"I know," she said, and the simplicity of the sentiment had momentarily stunned him.

"We can't yet," he said. "I'm a teacher here, technically. I want to ask you—" He stopped and started again. "I want to ask you to wait. But that's not fair. You're young and beautiful and popular..."

With a quick glance around first, Cassidy touched her finger to his lips to quiet him. "I've already been waiting," she said slowly. "Waiting for you to finally say this to me."

"Then why didn't you say it first?"

Cassidy laughed, a musical sound. "You've always known how I feel."

He clasped her hand. "On graduation day, we'll start—us. We'll graduate from the old us to the new us. We'll be something more. We'll—meet right here."

"I'll be here," Cassidy said. She leaned in until she was an inch from his lips, then pulled away. "Oops. I almost couldn't wait..."

"I can't wait to see what this guy is doing," Cassidy said.

Eric shook himself out of his reverie. He rubbed at both temples with his fingers, then looked where Cassidy was pointing. A man in front of them was setting up a folding table and chair, and he was dressed in red with a huge red paper heart taped to his shirt. He attached a cardboard sign to the table that read, Lovelife Advice. Whether U Want It or Not.

"Interesting," Eric said.

The man seated himself behind the table, but instead of waiting patiently for a taker, he launched into a kind of opening speech.

"Ladies and gentleman," he shouted, "I have been dumped."

A couple of passersby stopped and waited to see what would come next. Several government-protester fans turned around, also.

Eric looked at Cassidy, who raised one brow.

"My name is Rex, and I have been dumped," the man called, beating one fist on his chest. "And it was my own bloody fault."

"Somehow I don't doubt that," Eric whispered.

Cassidy chuckled. "Shh," she admonished.

"I was dumped," Rex repeated, "and if you asked me why—"

"Why?" Eric called. Cassidy shoved him in the arm.

"Glad you asked, mate," Rex retorted. "Though I would've told you anyhow. But here it is." He paused. *"Fear!"* he bellowed.

A toddler, walking with her father, froze at the sudden shout and stared goggle-eyed at the heartbroken man.

"Fear, that's all it was," Rex shouted to the world, which consisted of half a dozen onlookers now. "Fear of trusting, fear of the truth, fear of love. And now my love is *gone!*"

He didn't break down into sobs or anything like that. His words were raw, agonized, brutal, and they clutched at Cassidy's heart.

"I'm revealing myself to you, my good friends," Rex said, "because I have nothing left. I'm a broken man. And if I can keep someone else from making the same mistake, well, then, I won't feel as though I have to leap into the Thames."

"This guy's making me nervous," Eric whispered again, but Cassidy couldn't smile.

She stood. "Let's just go," she said, and Eric rose to his feet.

"You, there!" Rex called to Eric.

"Uh-oh," Eric mumbled to Cassidy, then raised his chin to acknowledge the brokenhearted man.

"Did I deserve to have my girlfriend leave me?" Rex demanded of Eric.

"Uh…"

"Speak up! What do you think?"

"Uh—yes?"

"Too right!" Rex looked delighted at what was really a depressing answer. "I deserved it. Now, mate, take a good look at me. Are you willing to become the pathetic creature I am?"

"Certainly not," Eric said with a grin, looking as though he was beginning to enjoy himself. Two female onlookers clapped.

"Right again!" Rex said. "Don't be a stupid fool

like me, if you want to hang on to that pretty girl of yours."

Cassidy pushed Eric forward to leave. He moved closer to Rex's table to walk around it. "Good luck to you," Eric said.

"My luck's run out. But many thanks, all the same, for your care and concern."

Cassidy followed Eric but as she was about to pass by Rex, he turned his head. She stopped, struck by the bottomless despair—so familiar to her—she saw in his flat gray eyes.

"It's you," he said quietly, stepping close to her.

Eric was moving away from her, not realizing she'd been held up.

"It's you," Rex said, "who has the fear. Not your bloke there. I can tell. You're like me."

She flinched.

"Be strong," Rex urged, and tapped her upper arm. "Be strong and you'll live happily ever after."

Cassidy, struggling with her inability to move or to speak, didn't see Eric double back. "What's going on here?" he asked, the joviality gone from his face. "Is he bothering you?" he asked her.

She shook her head no and let Eric lead her away. She saw him cast a glare over his shoulder.

But Rex *had* been bothering her, bothering the ugly, gnarling thing in her that she'd managed to ignore for just a few hours. She knew this poor man's words were meant to comfort her, but they made her feel worse. She'd let her guard down so much with

Eric that even a perfect stranger could see through to her soul.

Despite the advice, she couldn't be strong about that. She felt like nothing but a weakling.

"Is that guy there every week?" Eric asked as they continued up Oxford Street.

"No."

"Did he say something to upset you?"

Cassidy took a deep breath. "I have to go."

Eric halted in place. "What? Why?"

"I have work to do today." She resisted the childish urge to cross her fingers behind her back. "Some things I need to do before work tomorrow."

"But…didn't we decide we need to feel our way through this?"

"I am. I will be."

His face fell. "Without me around, you mean."

For the first time in her life, Cassidy wanted desperately to scream, to yell her emotions to the sky, like Rex. She wanted to shout that Eric's presence made her forget everything but being with him. His piercing black eyes, his strong body, his smooth fingertips, his impossibly soft lips—he rendered her unable to think, and that was very dangerous.

"This isn't the end," she assured him. "I just really have to—"

"I'm sorry," he said. "I know your work's important."

She ignored the stab of guilt for her fib. "Maybe after work tomorrow, we can…we can…"

"Continue this," Eric finished for her.

"Yes," she whispered. Just not now, just not now… It was foolish but she had to go and be alone. She'd spent so many years alone that it was hard to not retreat to the aloneness in a moment like this, when she felt helpless to rescue herself.

Eric seemed very reluctant, but said, "Okay. Okay. But see me after work tomorrow. Please. We'll have dinner, go for a walk, anything you want. Whatever is transpiring here between us, I want to take it slow for you."

She noticed he didn't point out they didn't have much time before he returned to the U.S. She already had a feeling he'd stay if they felt it was the right step toward sorting themselves out.

Cassidy backed up a step, intending to turn and head for the Tube. But before she could, Eric reached out and placed his palm on the back of her neck. As if in slow motion, she could feel each finger touch and then remain on her skin, warming her.

He pulled her toward him and kissed her. It was a feather of a kiss, a light, quiet echo of the heated one in his hotel room.

When he took his hand and mouth back, her blood sizzled through her veins, so hot she could almost hear it crackling. Heat pooled in between her thighs.

"Let's meet at the pub where we ate after the bookstore," he said. "Whatever time you're done. I'll hang around until I see you. I have a good book to read while I wait." He smiled.

She nodded.

"See you tomorrow," he said in a voice as soft as their kiss had been.

She turned and headed for the subway. The kiss had left her light-headed, but she tried very hard to keep her balance, in case he was watching her walk away.

Chapter Nine

The whole next day, any time Ambassador Cole made an appearance in the front office, he was approached and quizzed by staffers, all of whom had heard over the weekend that he was all right but were relieved to see him for themselves.

Cassidy noticed the ambassador appeared tired, but otherwise his usual self. He'd told her that he took the opportunity to spend some quiet time with his girlfriend the previous day, and it had clearly done wonders for restoring his state of mind.

Ironically, Cassidy's time yesterday with her not-really-boyfriend had clearly done things to *her* state of mind, as well. Just not quite the same things. More like frenzied, fretful, flummoxing things.

She hadn't seen Eric yet today and she speculated if it was deliberate on her part. He was always able to read her better than anyone. He'd probably figured out her need for a time-out and would strategically reappear around quitting time.

As much thinking as she'd done in the last day, she still wasn't prepared to interact with him again. It had been her idea to feel things out and let things happen, but that didn't stop her from being nervous about it.

In the late afternoon the ambassador came into the front office and cleared his throat. For the benefit of those on calls and those deeply engrossed in work, Cassidy called, "People! Can we have your attention?"

When he had all the ears in the room, Ambassador Cole said, "I commend this staff for your hard work this past week. Each one of you, in every job you've done, has had a personal impact on this Northern Ireland peace initiative, and I am proud to work with such dedicated, amazing fellow Americans."

Cassidy saw Eric slip in the main door and slide unobtrusively into the corner.

The ambassador went on to laud the work of the diplomats sent by the State Department. When he was finished, he insisted everyone in the room applaud themselves.

The room exploded with cheers and Cassidy caught Eric's eye. She held out her hands to him and clapped harder. He grinned and did the same.

Cassidy had had many moments in her professional life when she'd taken a step back and realized how far she'd come. But this moment was a great achievement for her workplace, and she was beyond fortunate to share the glory with her oldest ally and friend.

In that moment the issues between them didn't matter. They were two kids who'd grown up together and had the opportunity to do something important for the world. When the applause in the room finally died down, Eric and Cassidy's claps lingered in the air.

"If you can knock off early, go ahead and do it," the ambassador said to everyone. "You deserve it."

He left the center of the room and staffers hurried to their desks, many already shutting down computers and donning jackets, eager to get a few extra hours to themselves. Cassidy was trying to decide whether she could do the same when she saw Ambassador Cole beckon to Eric. The two men disappeared in the direction of the diplomat's office and Cassidy was left with a furrowed brow.

"Eric, I want to personally thank you again for all your valuable work," the ambassador said. "Your insights were a great help to me."

"Thank you, Ambassador," Eric said, flattered. "I was honored to get a chance to work with you on a project of such immense significance."

"Will you be staying in London?"

"Sadly, no. I have a flight to Boston tomorrow night."

The ambassador sat back. The immense chair nearly swallowed him up. He studied Eric, and pressed his fingertips together in a way that reminded Eric of his grade school principal.

Finally the ambassador said, "If you decided that maybe you wanted to stay in London, I could make a few phone calls for you."

"That's very generous," Eric said, surprised. "But I don't anticipate needing to take advantage of your kindness."

"Right. Well, if you discover that maybe you have a good—" he cleared his throat "—*reason* to stay on here, I can try to help you out."

He looked deliberately out the large glass window and Eric followed his gaze as Cassidy hurried by, carrying a pile of file folders.

Eric snapped his head back to the ambassador, who was unfazed. *How did he know?* Eric wondered. Had he and Cassidy been that obvious in the embassy? He hadn't thought so.

"I know you're the political adviser," the ambassador said. "But maybe I'll try my hand at a little bit of advice of my own. Stick around. Explore your options for a while."

Eric realized he ought to play along. "I think I'd be taking a risk by not going home."

A smile teased the corner of the ambassador's mouth. "As you probably know by now from working with me, I don't tend to make a statement without solid evidence to back it up."

He's saying he knows Cassidy wants me. Eric still didn't know how, but then again, the wiser ambassador had been around Cassidy the last ten years, something fate had denied Eric.

"I won't keep you," Ambassador Cole said, standing. "I trust you'll let me know if you need anything."

"Of course. And my services are always available to you, as well."

"I'm glad for that." The ambassador's smile was wide and genuine.

The phone on his desk rang.

"Take care, sir," Eric said, closing the door.

"Ambassador Cole," he heard the man say into the receiver. Then Eric gathered his things and left the building. He wanted to change before meeting Cassidy at the pub.

Cassidy opened up the door. Her office was growing stuffy, but she was packing up to leave for the night anyhow. Her heart banged hard in her chest as she shoved her appointment book, thick with paper-clipped notes and business cards, into her briefcase. She couldn't help anticipating the evening ahead. All day, her mind had run a constant movie loop of she and Eric kissing in his hotel. She tried to be angry at herself for her anticipation, but the thought of more kisses that could lay ahead…or more…

They'd feel it out. Let it unfold. Was the future she'd thought she'd ruined possible, after all?

She heard a voice. "Everyone, may I please have your attention for a moment?"

Ambassador Cole? What could be going on that she didn't know about? That he didn't discuss with her first before addressing her staff? She grabbed a pen and legal pad and warily stepped into the front office.

One look at the ambassador's face unnerved her even more. He was drawn, his skin pale, his eyes so sad.

Something was very wrong.

The assembled group was much smaller than the one he'd spoken to just a little while ago, many having taken advantage of their boss's invitation to leave early. The people who were left looked bemused. Charles glanced at Cassidy and raised his brows. She shrugged back at him.

Ambassador Cole cleared his throat. "I'm deeply saddened to deliver this news to you all. I just had a phone call. Our co-worker, Sophie Messing, was killed this weekend in a car accident in America."

The floor wobbled underneath Cassidy as a blinding rush crashed through her brain. She felt herself stagger and hit a wall. *How? How?* "No," she said out loud.

The room was frozen for just a moment. Then several women started to cry. Charles's hands were on his head, gripping hard handfuls of his own hair.

"What happened?" someone sobbed.

"She was in a cab from the airport," the ambassador said, regaining his composure for his staff. "Another car went out of control and hit the cab."

People cried harder, sorrow thickening the air. Cassidy felt herself fall with a hard thud and realized she'd slid down the wall, her legs unable to hold her up. "No," she said again. "No, no, no…"

"I've seen many tragic events in my career," Ambassador Cole said, "but this— Sophie was a dedicated, wonderful, lovely person…"

He went on speaking, trying to comfort his staff the best he could, then began walking around the room to offer hugs and consolation to individuals.

Cassidy went to cover her face with her hands but her cheeks were too slippery with tears she hadn't realized had poured out of her. She stared at her wet palms.

Sophie? She was young, vibrant, full of life and love. Braver than Cassidy would ever be.

And now she was gone.

Cassidy didn't know how long she sat there, numbed cold by the news. Her boss eventually knelt by her side.

"Cassidy," the ambassador said. "I'm so sorry."

"Yes," she whispered.

"I noticed you and Sophie talking and laughing outside last week. Had you become good friends?"

She tried to say yes again, but her throat was stopped up.

"Do you recall my suggesting you should feel free to take a few days off if you needed it? Now's probably an appropriate time. Why don't you plan on a few days? Call me whenever you're ready."

Cassidy tried to cough the lump away. "Other people might want time off..." she protested in a weak, thin voice.

"We'll manage. We'll be all right. Just go. Try to relax."

The diplomat took hold of her shoulder and her elbow and helped her to her feet before moving to another staff member and murmuring condolences.

Cassidy hadn't even wanted Sophie to go back to the United States. Not after her new friend had told her she'd been planning to spill her damaging secret to her fiancé. Had she at least had the chance she'd wanted to unburden herself, to come clean, before she—

No, Cassidy realized. She died on the way home from the airport. She'd said she was going to write a letter on the plane. Ken didn't know the truth.

Cassidy felt a momentary flash of relief, but it was over before it had begun. What had Sophie said to her? *If I live day after day with him without giving him a chance to learn the real me, that will hurt much deeper… When you trust people, it gives them the fullest opportunity to understand you. And care about you.*

Sophie was different than Cassidy. And Cassidy had a feeling that if Sophie had foreseen that she wouldn't live, she would have wanted Ken to know the truth anyway, so that at least he could mourn the real her. That he could miss who she truly was.

Cassidy's resolve pierced like a sword through the fog of her brain. She lurched on still-noodly legs to Sophie's desk and scanned her personal things. A Hello Kitty stapler. A pile of plastic Mardi Gras-style bead necklaces. A photo, taken near Big Ben, of Sophie with her arms around an older version of her—probably her mother. Cassidy realized that she'd never have the opportunity to ask Sophie about the photo. Her eyes filled up. She brushed the back of her hand hard across her eyes and moved a pile of papers. There. Sophie's Rolodex.

Cassidy flipped through frantically, cards sticking together in her rush to find what she needed. She got to the end with no luck. She started at the beginning A's again and ordered herself to concentrate.

She found it in the middle of the deck. "Ken—home, Ken—cell, Ken—work."

Cassidy pulled the card out and examined it. It was bright white and stiff. Barely handled. Of course. Sophie would know these numbers from memory. Cassidy was grateful for whatever it was that drove Sophie to write these numbers down anyhow. Probably just the girlish pleasure of putting her lover's name in print.

Cassidy palmed the card, ran to her office for her things, and flew out the door without pausing to put on her coat.

"May I speak to Ken, please?"

An older woman with a sad voice had answered at Ken's home number. "I don't know if he can—" she began haltingly.

"Please, ma'am," Cassidy interrupted. "My name is Cassidy Maxwell and I was a—" she swallowed "—I was Sophie's friend. May I please speak to Ken?"

There was a pause as the woman considered. "Hold on," she said. Cassidy listened to muffled voices in the background, male and female.

She fought her physical urge to hang up, to leave everything alone. She'd spent so many years hiding her own nasty secrets under wraps that her body was actually warring with her now—her brain screaming at her to hang up, her hands shaking so badly it was hard to hold the phone, her heart beating so hard it threatened to rip out of her. Sitting on the sofa, she pulled her knees to her chest, pressing, trying to control herself.

Poor Sophie had been about to do this of her own free will, so Cassidy pushed back against her own soul to keep her courage for just a few minutes more.

"Hello?" she finally heard, and it broke her heart. It was a man, a man so racked with agony that his voice was ragged and empty.

"Hello, Ken," she began. "My name is Cassidy Maxwell. I worked with Sophie."

"You were her boss," he said, but there was no emotion in the recognition, only statement of fact. "She mentioned you."

"We recently became very friendly." She paused. "I want to offer you my deepest sympathies for your terrible loss." This was difficult. She wasn't very good at finding words in everyday situations. Finding words in this tragic situation was almost impossible. "She was wonderful."

"Yes," Ken said, and his voice broke on a sob. "She was."

Cassidy waited a few moments for Ken to compose himself. "Ken. I called for one more reason. Sophie—Sophie was going to give you something when she returned. A…a letter."

"A letter? From who?"

"From herself. She was going to write you a letter."

"Why?"

Cassidy's throat closed up. What was she doing? She didn't know Sophie's secret. Talking to Ken could be a huge mistake.

She was about to hang up with just her condolences when Sophie's recent words came back to her. "This is right for me, even if you think it isn't right for you."

Cassidy was Sophie's friend, and it wasn't her place to judge Sophie's decision. It was her obligation to carry out Sophie's wish.

She cleared her stopped-up throat and summoned the strength to follow through. "I wouldn't have bothered you at a terrible time like this, but a few days ago, Sophie told me she was going to write you a letter and it was—crucially important to her that you read it."

She took Ken's silence as a sign to continue. "I personally don't know the contents of the letter. It's meant for you alone. But she said she was going to write it on the plane trip home. The letter may be in her purse or her carry-on bag. It might be best for you to wait a while until you're, um, strong enough to read it, but I wanted to make sure you're aware of its existence."

Ken's silence went on even longer, and Cassidy was just beginning to worry that he'd been overwhelmed and her words had been completely lost on him when he spoke. "I'll…I'll look for it."

"Ken? Sophie loved you. So, so much. And she was looking forward to her future with you."

She heard a sound that could have been a sob or a small laugh. "I know," he said, and Cassidy smiled through her own sorrow. Of course he knew. Sophie wasn't the kind of woman who'd keep her love to herself.

"Thank you, Cassidy," she heard, and didn't have time to say goodbye when he softly hung up.

Cassidy laid her cheek against her knees and stared out her window, where the sky was post-midnight-black. Keeping the time difference in mind, she'd stayed awake to try not to call Ken's home when he might be eating dinner. Though she guessed that he probably wouldn't have been eating at all.

Calling Ken and fulfilling Sophie's last mission had been necessary, but terrifying. Telling her own secrets would be even more terrifying, but luckily wasn't quite as necessary.

She had let herself be taken in by Eric. By her memories of him, and by the way he was now—the way he smiled, the way he kissed.

The phone rang, for probably the thirteenth time in the past four hours. And for the thirteenth time, she didn't answer it. About three hours ago, her door buzzer had startled her. She'd sat silently on her living room floor as it buzzed four times, with about five minutes between each. Then it had stopped.

Now, Cassidy picked up the phone cradle and turned the ringer off. She couldn't bear Eric's constant reminders that she had stood him up.

She felt bad about being rude. But not bad enough. She had let her guard down around him. She knew if she saw him again, she would let down her guard again. She wasn't safe, her secrets weren't safe, whenever she was with him.

So, it was time to get away from him.

And she knew just where to go.

She leaped off the sofa and hurried the few steps to

her bedroom. She dragged her suitcase out from under her bed, her feet in socks sliding on the hardwood floor as she did so. She laid the bag on her bed, unzipped it, then opened several dresser drawers.

She'd go, be alone, wait until Eric flew back to Boston, back to a corner of her mind labeled "past." Then she'd come back and start over again. She knew she could do that. She knew she was good at it.

Eric dragged himself out of bed two hours before his 8:00 a.m. wake-up call. There was no point in staying in bed if you weren't sleeping. But the tossing and turning and worrying had left him crusty-eyed and heavy-headed.

He sat in his desk chair. A streak of weak new daylight shot in between the thick drapes, illuminating the newly clean room. His long, almost-continuous time here had transformed this impersonal room into a personal headquarters for him. But last night, after the cold realization that Cassidy was back to having nothing to do with him, Eric had used his angry energy to pack everything up for tonight's flight home.

He felt like an idiot, calling and calling her, going to her apartment and buzzing her. He had vowed not to feel like this about her again. But dammit, he did, and even more so than before, and this time he wasn't going to give up without a fight.

A light had been on at her flat, and he'd seen a shadow pass behind her curtain at one point before he'd first buzzed, so at least he knew she was physically safe.

He would have preferred to *see* her safe, to feel her safe in his arms…

He closed his eyes to experience the image better, and woke up two hours later with his head bent back at a painful angle, hanging over the backrest of the chair.

He threw himself onto the rumpled and now-cold bed, and stared at the phone for a few moments. Well, it wasn't as if he had any pride left. He dialed the main embassy number, had himself put through to administration, and had a secretary inform him that Cassidy Maxwell would not be in the office for the next few days.

Eric sat back against the pillows, perplexed. Granted, he hadn't worked with Cassidy very long, but it was long enough to ascertain that she was a woman who didn't miss work, even if they had to wheel her into her office on a stretcher.

Eric was dressed, out the door and walking up Cassidy's street in record time, thanks to more frequent rush-hour Tube trains. He raised his hand to buzz her flat when the door was kicked open and a paint-splattered worker emerged, rushing down the stairs.

Eric examined the lobby mailboxes and figured out Cassidy was on the second floor. He climbed one flight of stairs. There was a dropcloth, a few paintbrushes and a square aluminum tin on the floor at the top.

He stood at the door to Cassidy's flat. The paint was chipping a bit over the doorknob. At eye level was a little brass cat hanging by its tail, the sign proclaiming Welcome. The cute cat seemed like something bought for Cassidy by her mother.

He rapped on the door, perhaps a little too hard, judging by the sting in his knuckles. "Cassidy? Please, it's Eric."

No answer. He was wondering if he should attempt to find the landlord to make sure she was all right when the worker from downstairs came thudding up the stairs slowly, carrying two buckets of paint in each hand. His shoulders slumped from the weight.

Eric bent and pushed the dropcloth, brushes and tin aside so the worker wouldn't have to step over them. "Cheers, mate," the man said, and set the cans down. "If you're looking for Ms. Maxwell," he added, "you missed her about a half hour ago."

Eric furrowed his brow. Huh? If she wasn't en route to work, where was she off to at this hour? Unless she was sick, maybe? "Did she…did she look all right?"

"Ms. Maxwell always looks good, eh?" the man said, grunting as he crouched on the floor to pry a lid off one can. "I'm glad she's not here. I haven't seen her around lately to tell her I was painting all the doors today. Now she won't have to put up with the fumes."

Eric stood there for a few minutes more, trying to figure out where to go next. Maybe the pastry place across the street? Then the bookstore? He didn't really know where else she hung out.

The painter lifted his sandy blond head. "You still here? Do me a favor, then." He got to his feet with a groan, plucked the Welcome cat off the door and handed it to Eric. "Hold this for Ms. Maxwell? I need to paint the door and I don't know where to leave it, since she's not coming back for a few days..."

"What? How do you know that?"

"Well, by the suitcase I carried down the stairs for her. It was heavy enough for a long trip, but you know the way women pack. Maybe she'll be back tomorrow."

"Where was she going?" Eric demanded.

The painter, not in the least intimidated, cocked a brow. "Didn't know and didn't ask. Maybe she was running away." The curious expression on his face finished the sentiment. *Running away from you?*

Eric tucked the door hanger into his inside coat pocket. "Thanks," he said, dashing down the stairs and out the door. But when the cool air hit him, he stopped. The whole world was out there, and Cassidy had gone out into it with a suitcase.

She could be anywhere.

Eric headed to the only place he could think of. A place that was built to assist wayward Americans like himself.

The embassy.

Luckily, the ambassador was on the premises. In a matter of minutes, Eric was sitting in his office.

"What can I do for you?" Ambassador Cole asked.

Desperation overrode Eric's usual need to be discreet about his personal affairs. "Well," he said, "I was thinking yesterday that perhaps I do have a reason to stay in London for a while."

"Yes?" the older man prompted, appearing encouraged.

"But suddenly I seem to have lost my reason for staying."

The ambassador seemed confused.

"I mean, literally," Eric clarified. "I lost it. I lost her. I can't find Cassidy anywhere. We were supposed to meet, and— I just need to know if she's okay."

Ambassador Cole took a deep breath. "One of her co-workers, Sophie, was killed in a car crash in America a few days ago."

Eric was stunned. Cute, young Sophie? Cassidy's friend? "When—?"

"I got the call yesterday right after you left. A lot of people took it hard. I gave Cassidy some time off."

Eric felt the air leave his body, deflating him. What a blow, to lose a friend. He wished Cassidy would have let him—be there for her. Support her, do something for her. He ached with wanting to go to her. "I called her a thousand times. I went to her place. I have to know if she's all right."

"I talked to her this morning."

Eric was relieved, but he couldn't help the thought that clicked across his brain. *Why didn't she call me?*

"Physically, she's fine," the ambassador added. "Emotionally, well, she's quite fragile."

"I need to—" Eric began and stopped.

"So this is not just a concerned inquiry about her overall health. You want to know if I know where she is, so you can go find her."

No use denying it. That would just waste time. "Right."

"I see." The ambassador studied him a moment. "If

she hasn't contacted you herself, then perhaps she doesn't want to see you."

"She said that?"

"I feel comfortable coming to that conclusion."

Eric sighed.

"I care about Cassidy. She's nearly family," Ambassador Cole added. "I wouldn't want to go against her wishes.

"Then again, I am a bit older than her," he continued, "and I have been around the block a few more times. If I sat and considered it a while, perhaps I would decide to go against what she wants and do what I believe is best for her."

Eric leaned forward with expectation.

"However," the diplomat said, "I don't have time to sit and consider it a while. I have an extra-busy day ahead of me today, thanks to the un-Cassidy-like inefficiency of her temporary stand-in."

Eric exhaled slowly and stood, putting out his hand.

The ambassador grasped it, then pulled Eric close to speak low into his ear. "Did I ever tell you about my summer cottage in Brighton?"

Huh? Why would he think Eric could care about this now? "No, uh, you haven't."

"Pretty little cottage right on the water there. All the way down the side road after the Salty Goose pub. Last cottage in the row there. Dark green."

Eric nodded politely, having no clue what to say.

"I keep up the utilities even in the cooler weather," the ambassador said, walking Eric to the door. "And I have people in to clean regularly. In case I need to travel out there spur-of-the-moment. It's the perfect place to get away. If you need some time alone, to think."

Before the man could get his last word out, Eric realized the value of this information. Cassidy.

Cassidy was there.

"My closest associates know they're welcome there any time they need it," the ambassador said casually.

"That sounds like the perfect place," Eric said, his excitement building.

"It is. I must have told you about it." The ambassador opened the door.

"Probably just slipped my mind," Eric said before he slipped out the door.

Chapter Ten

Dear Mr. Broadstreet,

I am writing this letter in support of Professor Gilbert Harrison. It has come to my attention that...

Dear Mr. Broadstreet,

I am writing this letter in protest of the recent action taken by the Saunders University board against Professor Gilbert Harrison...

Mr. Broadstreet,

Are you insane or merely stupid? Professor Gilbert Harrison is an academic role model for students, and yet you want to fire him. As an alum,

I must say I can't believe you'd try to deprive Saunders students of his outstanding influence. If you're so gung-ho about firing someone, where the hell were you ten years ago when Randall Greene, a disgusting monster of a sexual predator, enjoyed a position on the faculty…

Cassidy crumpled up the thirty-eighth letter she'd started and chucked it in the trash. She'd better get it right or soon she'd be out of paper and ink. But she couldn't get it right. Every letter she tried to write on Gilbert's behalf either sounded bland and standard, or a crazy rant full of rage and revulsion. Neither style would help the professor's case.

However, this had to be finished today. She'd kept putting if off this week, but she realized that getting it written, coupled with Eric leaving the country tonight, would free her. To start over.

Again.

She rolled the soft leather executive chair away from the handsome, ornate writing desk. Upon arriving at the ambassador's Brighton dwelling, she'd made herself at home. The "cottage" was not the quaint type you'd see lining the edge of the Atlantic on the Jersey Shore. If you pushed about three and a half of those together and piled them two high, you'd get this one. It was the last in a long line of big cottages, and surrounded with enough land that Cassidy guessed even in the touristy summer, this remained a haven of peace and quiet.

No one would find her here.

The coastal wind whistled against the picture window and rain began to slap hard against the glass. Cassidy looked out into the blackness. It was hard to believe the vastness of the invisible waters were so near, when she could only see her own reflection from the desk lamp. Her yellow satin pajamas shimmered.

She'd brought books with her, but couldn't concentrate on deciphering sentences. TV was bearable for less than an hour. She'd tried to nap. She'd even tried meditating, piling lush pillows on the floor and sitting among them, but her brain refused to go silent. It was all Eric, all the time.

She'd hoped this self-imposed isolation might cleanse her mind and rid her body of the physical imprint of him. But no—thoughts of every chronological moment since he'd stepped foot in London marched through her head and when they arrived to the present day, they circled back to the beginning and started over again.

This had happened last time, too. Ten years ago, when she'd last pulled the Cassidy Maxwell Disappearing Act. The Eric memory brigade had tormented her then, too, as she lay in bed, willing the painkillers to numb him away. But they didn't, no matter how many she tossed back.

Then one day a woman had knocked on her door, the door to that ratty apartment that Cassidy hated. The woman came out of the blue. She wouldn't reveal how she'd known about Cassidy, but she promised to help her kick the meds to the curb. Faced with the job offer in London that was the answer to her prayers, Cassidy let her in. Their association had been brief but effective—by then, Cassidy was motivated. So motivated, in fact, that she hadn't wasted time wondering how the counselor had found her. And when she got to London, she'd embarked on blocking out all her Massachusetts memories, and the counselor was included in those things she didn't think about anymore.

But now that she was thinking about them…about all of it—

The mysterious drug counselor. The out-of-nowhere job offer.

And what had Eric said? A benefactor. Gilbert Harrison had been acting on behalf of a rich benefactor.

Could it be? Could this benefactor have gotten Cassidy the plum job, gotten her off the drugs?

And—could he have also been behind Randall Greene's eventual and richly deserved punishment?

The more she considered it now, the more convinced she became that it was true. A stab of remorse ripped through her chest for Gilbert. Somehow, some mystery friend of his had saved her life. Meanwhile, Gilbert was now going through purgatory. It would tear him apart if he lost that job. She remembered his unparalleled passion for teaching. She also remembered learning the bomb of a secret he'd been hiding—an overheard conversation, a peek at a file. He was in a bad position now. Years of covering up could lead to a blow-up, and in the public eye. He would be hurt, as well as another person, whose identity Cassidy just happened to know.

But what could she do for Gilbert now? Write one hell of a letter? Was that enough?

She had to figure something out for him. A letter might not help him now—Eric was right about that.

Eric.

Oh, God.

The last time she saw him—the two of them applauding one another. It was appropriate. It would have to do as her last memory of him.

She and Eric had been tempted to pick up where they'd left off, but there was no denying this was now many years later. They were different people, older people.

Coming clean about her past was the right decision for Sophie. After all, she was going to marry Ken. But it was a different situation altogether for Cassidy.

It wasn't as if Eric was really in love with her anymore.

A tear slipped out of her eye but she didn't bother to wipe it away. Between Sophie's tragedy and leaving Eric again, weeping was becoming an every-hour-on-the-hour event. She tried again to look out at the water and again saw only herself in the window, this time with a tear illuminated like a sharp crystal against her cheek.

A knock on the door almost made her crash through the glass. She whirled around. It wasn't particularly late, but the beach was deserted in this weather, at this time of year.

Her gaze darted around the room and she picked up a letter opener on the desk. Well, she was having about the worst week of her life. If some homicidal lunatic was trying the my-car-broke-down-can-I-use-your-phone-trick, he was in for a surprise.

Another knock, harder and with more raps. This time she thought she heard a voice. She slipped from the den and headed into the front room, then the foyer, where she could hear better. The rain sounded louder.

"Cassidy!" she heard. "Cassidy!"

Right. Not likely a homicidal lunatic would know her by name. But the ambassador certainly would. He hadn't mentioned he was planning to stay here, but probably he came to the area to visit his girlfriend and was dropping by to see if Cassidy was all right.

She tossed the letter opener onto a side table. The pouring rain muffled any identifying characteristics in her boss's voice, but, she thought as she slid over the chain and turned the knob, there was no one else who would show up here who just happened to know she was here, also.

She opened the door.

"Cassidy."

Eric stood there in front of her.

His soaked hair slicked down into points all around his face and raindrops clung to his eyelashes. His light blue cotton sweater under his open coat was molded wetly against his chest. His black, black eyes locked on to hers.

How—why— How could he—

Several minutes ticked by. A gust of wind blew a smattering of dampness onto Cassidy's lips and forehead. She shivered, resigned.

Finally, Eric spoke.

"You ran away from me," he said. "You ran away from us. Once is quite enough, Cassidy. I'm not going to let you do this again."

Cassidy stared. She found her voice, but it betrayed her by stammering. "Wh-Why? How…how did you find me?"

"Why?" he repeated. "Did you think I'd just forget about you? Then? And now?"

She didn't answer.

"You're as good at hiding as when you were a kid," he said. "But you remember what I told you then, don't you?"

Cassidy shook her head and realized the rest of her body was shaking, too.

"No matter how long it takes, all you have to do is wait. I'll figure out where you are. I'll always come to get you."

Those long-forgotten words, emerging now in his deep, sexy, man's voice, made Cassidy weak. And although she possibly should have been preparing her whole life to hear it, it jolted her being like an electrical shock when he added, "Because I love you."

"I—I—" She tried to answer.

Then she fell into his arms.

In their rush, their mouths met in a bruising crush. Their hands clutched and grabbed and clung all over. Cassidy felt Eric's strong hands pressing a wet trail up her spine, warming her even as the cold rain lashed through her hair. She surrendered to the elements, to the night, to the only man she'd ever wanted. He licked his way from her jaw to her collarbone, and Cassidy threw her head back and cried out. Eric slid his palms from her shoulders down to her breasts, running his thumb over the hardened buds underneath the thin satin. She arched her back, pressing into his touch. He moaned, then swept her up into his arms.

He stepped into the foyer and slammed the door with his foot. Cassidy put her hands behind his neck, pulled him down and kissed him deeply. Their progress was halted as she traced the shape of his lips with her tongue. She felt him stagger back, then regain his control. He dragged his mouth away from hers and peered over her shoulder to find his way into the living room, where Cassidy had earlier built a small fire in the fireplace and lit several candles on the mantel. A flickering glow filled the room.

He set her down on her feet in front of him and she forced herself to still and look into his eyes. In the absence of light, they were an opaque onyx. They had a lusty glaze to them now. Her breath caught. She'd been literally waiting for this moment for a decade. She hadn't let one man touch her, see her, since coming to London.

She'd never wanted anyone but Eric.

He didn't move. She knew he longed to.

She reached out with both hands and pushed his wet coat onto the floor. She tugged his soaked sweater over his head, throwing it into a pile on the floor behind him. He kicked off his shoes as she did so, then stopped, apparently willing to let her take the lead.

His torso was beautiful and toned, his upper arms muscular. The firelight threw defining shadows over the masculine planes and angles and soft-looking dark hair.

She locked eyes with him again. *He always knows*

what I'm thinking, she thought. *Even now.* She transmitted a challenge through her gaze. She unbuttoned her pajama top, took a deep breath and let it slip from her shoulders and away from her body.

She wore nothing underneath.

But he wouldn't tear his eyes from hers. Not while she had him captive there. *Read my mind,* she thought at him. *You know how I feel, don't you?*

He didn't blink. But in the dim light, using her peripheral vision, she could see his bottom lip trembling. He wanted to see her.

Never wavering, she pushed the pajama pants off her hips. When they fell to her knees, she lifted one bare foot and pulled them all the way to the floor. She stepped away from the fabric, kicked it to the side. All the while, always staring.

His face was tight, tense. He silently begged, pleaded.

She made him wait one more moment, so he could read one more wordless thought.

I love you, too.

Then she slowly closed her eyes. She felt him finally surveying the visual landscape of her body, felt his heat radiating onto her skin. The first touch of his fingertips sent a swirling into her core and down between her thighs. That place throbbed and pulsed in a way that had been unfamiliar for a long, long time. Her entire body shuddered with the sensation.

He took his hands away and she opened her eyes long enough to see him slide his jeans down, taking his briefs and socks with them.

Their whole lives, Cassidy and Eric had known no one else better than each other, but now, naked and breathing heavily, there was much that had never been explored.

They wrapped their arms around each other, and as all of her skin pressed against all of his, they both sighed with relief. Together they sank to the thick wine-colored Oriental rug.

Eric eased her onto her back and bent over her body, closing his mouth over one nipple. Cassidy bucked upward at the sudden pleasure. He teased her skin with his tongue, catching the tip gently between his teeth, and when she could barely stand it anymore, he shifted to her other breast and did the same.

He kissed his way past the hollow of her midriff and she propped herself up on her elbows to watch him, involuntarily gasping as he touched and retreated, touched and retreated, moving lower and lower. Her body was luminescent and perspiring in the light and heat of the fire. Eric ran a finger through the small strip of curls at her center and she gasped. He flicked the tiny bud inside her folds, over and over. Then he parted the skin around it, lowered his head, and drew it between his lips.

A cry of need escaped her throat as he sucked and licked. He ran a hand down her inner thigh, down her calf, and lifted her leg so it draped over his shoulder and down his strong back. Then he slid the hand up to her breast again, squeezing her nipple between two fingers.

Never before had she felt anything like this. The sensation built, it built, it built, until she came to a pounding, throbbing explosion. Every cell in her body let go, every thought in her head dissolved.

A fire crackle snapped her out of her momentary reverie. Eric was leaning over her. She smoothed her palms down his sides and gripped his buttocks firmly in both hands. Then she pulled him down onto her.

"Cassidy," he breathed, and her name in her ear thrilled her. "Cassidy, only you…"

She pulled him to her and parted her legs. She brought one hand around to his front and closed over his hard length. He gasped and grabbed her wrist. "No. If you touch me, I'll—I need you, I need…"

She stretched her arms over her head. His hand still encircled her wrist. He took hold of the other one and looked into her eyes in a repeat of her earlier challenge. She didn't blink, either.

He penetrated her slowly, and with each small push, his face went a little slacker in ecstasy. She savored the feeling of his filling her completely, the feeling of her so tight around him.

When he was buried inside her, he stilled a moment. Cassidy lifted her head and kissed him.

He began to thrust, gently at first, then harder and harder. Her heels dug into the luxurious rug as he drove into her, and her movements matched his. She wrapped her legs around him, crossing her ankles. She felt his lower back muscles go taut again and again as they pushed against each other. The friction pushed her again to the edge and her hands over her head clenched into fists, signaling Eric to follow her into sweet release. He sighed out her name and his body grew heavy on hers. She wrapped her arms around his back, pulling her onto him, supporting him.

The pulsing inside her slowly subsided, and at the same time, she realized the rain outside was tapering off. She could now hear the hypnotic, repetitive roar of the surf, so close to them.

She smoothed a hand over his hair, which had air-dried to softness. They lay there for a long time, Cassidy watching light patterns dance on the ceiling, Eric's face in the hollow of her neck.

"Cassidy."

She shifted a little, angling her head to see his face.

"I want to tell you that I don't care anymore about what happened ten years ago."

Cassidy was confused.

"I mean," he said, "it doesn't matter anymore. I don't need to know why you left me. I won't ever ask you again. It's in the past. We've been given another chance to be together. Now is what's important." He lifted a hand, brushed a lock of hair from her forehead. "This moment."

He stroked her cheek, and Cassidy, trembling with the meaning of what he'd just said, the freedom he'd given her, gently pushed his arms aside and stood up. She went into the guest room she had claimed and returned with two pillows and a quilt. When they were settled back in, face-to-face, legs intertwined, she said softly, "I love you."

He smiled a luminous smile and kissed her, his lips lingering on hers even as his eyes closed.

He fell asleep. She lay awake for hours. Both were at peace.

When Eric awoke, he was alone.

Remembering he was not alone when he fell asleep, he sat up with a start. Morning sun had transformed the room from sparkling and magical to sharp and real. He smelled the now-dead fire and a chill ran through him.

Where was Cassidy?

Running. Running again…

He lurched onto his feet, swaying from the sleep that hadn't left him yet. He retrieved his damp jeans from the floor and yanked them on. Not bothering to button them, he glanced around, then headed down a hallway. There were a lot of rooms for a beach cottage. All empty rooms.

He tried not to panic, but his mind was reeling, wondering where he'd have to chase her to now.

His heart sinking, he pushed open the door to the last room and found Cassidy, dressed in jeans and a pink cardigan sweater, quietly but purposefully packing her suitcase.

He leaned against the door frame. She looked up, startled. "Oh," she said. "You're up."

"Oh," he repeated. "I can't believe this."

"I tried not to wake you."

"I'm sure."

She raised an eyebrow as he continued, "I'm sure waking me didn't fit into your master plan of running away again."

Her shoulders slumped and she shook her head. She

didn't say anything for a long time. Then she said, "We need to go to the airport now."

"Cassidy, please…"

"Weren't you supposed to fly back to Boston last night?"

He ran his hands through his sleep-tousled hair. "Yes. But I came here."

"I know. So we're going to the airport to get you another ticket. Hopefully we can get two seats together."

Eric stared.

"I'm going with you," Cassidy said. "We're going back to Saunders."

Relief flooded through Eric and he almost ran to her, gathering her up. "I'm sorry. I thought—"

She pulled away and cupped his face in her hands. "I know what you thought. But I'm making you a promise. I'm never running away from you again. Please believe me."

He held her. "I believe you." He kissed her and she kissed him back, and they fell onto the bed in a tangle, laughing. He reached for her.

"No," Cassidy said. "Seriously. The earlier we get to the airport, the better our chances are for getting a flight today. How did you get here, anyway?"

"Rented a car. I almost crashed about ninety-eight times on the way. Wrong side of the road and all."

Cassidy giggled. "I think I'll drive us back," she offered.

"Good idea. Thank you," he said, "for doing this. It means a lot to me. It will mean so much for Gilbert."

She sobered and worry creased her face. "I'm doing

this for several reasons. There are a few things I have to do. I hope when we get there—you'll understand."

"Whatever you need," he said, kissing her ear.

"I love you," Cassidy said. "I'm doing the right thing because of it."

"The right thing would be letting me unbutton this pretty little sweater and letting me…"

"We're leaving," Cassidy said, giving up a smile again. "If you cooperate, I'll let you unbutton my pretty little sweater in a Massachusetts motel."

Sounded good to him. A whole lot more than good.

Chapter Eleven

"Ambassador Cole."

"Ambassador, it's Cassidy."

"Ah," he said. "How are you doing?"

"I'm…all right. But I'm calling to extend my couple of days off to a couple of weeks. Is that…is that all right?"

"Of course. Take all the time you need. I believe this might be the first two-week vacation you've ever had in our employ, so I won't quibble about the bloody short notice." He chuckled, then fell silent, and in that silence was a question that Cassidy felt compelled to answer.

"I'm going back to Massachusetts. I have to…help out an old friend."

"I see. And you'll also be accompanied by an old friend?"

"As if you don't know," she teased. "Somehow I doubt Eric conducted a door-to-door search in Brighton to find me."

"I *was* in an uncertain political situation there," the ambassador admitted. "I had to use all my available information to make the correct move. Did I?"

Cassidy looked across the airport waiting area to the newsstand, where Eric was buying gum and two sodas. He smiled at the young clerk behind the counter, who giggled at him. Cassidy smiled, too. "For now, I think stability has been established," she said. "Thank you."

"You're very welcome."

She shifted from one foot to the other. "I must say I am concerned, though, about not being there to help you if the peace initiative heats up again."

"Cassidy," the ambassador said. "There has been unrest in Northern Ireland for decades. Whether or not my peace plan is accepted, nothing's going to be resolved in two weeks' time."

"What if it doesn't go through?" Cassidy asked, then wished she hadn't. Not once in the whole time the ambassador had been developing his peace plan had she expressed any worries. It was her job to work for change, not doubt its possibility. But talking to the ambassador now, at this moment, she couldn't help feeling he wouldn't mind her honesty.

"Well," he answered, "if it doesn't go through, we'll roll up our sleeves and try again."

"But it was so much work—"

"No. Peace is a never-ending process," he reminded

her. "If peace was restored there, it would be brilliant, but there's always another part of the world to examine, to assist. There's always work."

Cassidy sighed. "Yes, but it would just be so hard to see it fail."

The diplomat laughed a soft laugh, one that was filled with years of worldly experience. "There are no failures, just small trip-ups on the way to setting things right."

"If I've never told you, Ambassador Cole," Cassidy said, "it's an honor of the highest sort to work for you."

"And if I've never told you, Cassidy Maxwell," the ambassador said, "it's an honor of the highest sort to work *with* you." He cleared his throat. "Good luck helping your friend. Have a safe flight."

They bid goodbye and Cassidy hung up just as Eric came over to her. He handed her a can of Coke and offered her a stick of cinnamon gum. She declined with a wistful smile.

"Did the ambassador give you the okay?" he asked.

She nodded. She knew he would, but she'd wanted to hear his voice to make sure it was really all right.

Eric wrapped an arm around her and hugged her close, and she put her own arm around his waist, reveling in his warmth, wondering how she'd lived so long without it. Wondering if she'd have to, once she got to Saunders and did what she'd have to do.

The flight attendant called their row for boarding, and Cassidy shrugged into a backpack and picked up her suitcase. She grabbed Eric's hand with her free one.

"Are you a nervous flier?" Eric asked.

"No."

"Too bad. I was kind of hoping you'd be clutching on to me for the next eight hours."

Cassidy grinned. "I'll clutch on to you for eight hours after the flight, if you like."

"Oh, I like." He bent down and kissed her, his tongue sliding around hers. Someone behind them cleared their throat and they quickly separated and hurried ahead in line.

Eric steered the small rental car out of Logan International Airport and followed the signs for Storrow Drive. "It's weird to drive normally again."

Cassidy looked nervous.

Eric laughed. "I'm just kidding. I'm fine. Actually, I'm wide awake. I could drive us straight to Saunders right now. You can take a nap on the way. We can get a room off campus and go visit Gilbert in the morning. I forgot to call him, but that's okay. I'm sure it will be a surprise for him to see you."

"I'm sure it will," Cassidy murmured. She shifted in her seat, a bit uneasily, Eric realized. "Um," she said. "Let's stop on the way and continue in the morning."

"I really don't mind driving now."

"Nah. Why the rush?"

"Why the delay?" As soon as the words left his mouth, he remembered other words, words she'd said to him in London about not ever setting foot at Saunders again.

"I just want to be together," she said.

"We'll be together at Saunders," he said. "I promise."

He wasn't sure why he had to promise it, but had a feeling he was supposed to.

Cassidy was silent, staring out the front window at the road ahead. They had hit rush hour and Boston was in its typical gridlock. "Thank you," he heard her say.

"You're welcome," he replied. "And considering this traffic mess, I think your idea is the better one, after all. Shout when you see the first exit with a motel."

Cassidy's hand snaked along the seat and landed on his thigh. "I'll make it worth your while."

Eric cursed the fool drivers all around him, who had no idea what they were keeping him from.

Eric didn't give Cassidy a chance to lift even one shirt out of her open suitcase before he came up behind her and enveloped her in an embrace. He felt her relax beneath him, letting out a contented sigh. She leaned her head back on his shoulder as he kissed his way through her hair to nibble on her earlobe.

"Last time we were in a hotel room together," he whispered, his hands fumbling blind for her top button, "I vowed not to touch you unless you touched me first. Tonight, I'm not bothering with that courtesy. I hope you don't mind."

She sighed again. "How forward."

"Damn right."

"Were you…were you like this with all your girlfriends?"

The unexpected question stilled Eric in mid-nibble. He pulled his arms away and turned her around. He scrutinized her face. "Excuse me for saying so," he said, "but that was the most insecure thing I've ever, in my life, heard out of you."

Cassidy blushed, the bloom in her cheeks clashing with her auburn locks. "Maybe I am a…a little insecure," she mumbled.

"Why? This is right. Finally. We're where we're supposed to be." He smiled to reassure her.

She still appeared troubled, gnawing at her lower lip. "I haven't been any 'way' with other girlfriends," he confessed. "What I mean is, I never wanted one around long enough to be any kind of way."

"No, don't tell me—"

"I want you to know this. I never got close to any woman, after you. Not as close as I was with you. Partly because—" Eric swallowed "—my heart was so ripped open and I never wanted to hurt that badly again. But also partly because I knew I couldn't be as close to any woman who wasn't you. I even tried to date some nice women, women you'd like." He shook her shoulder in jest and she cracked a ghost of a smile.

"But no one lasted more than about two weeks," he went on. "It wasn't really fair to them. Not one ever had a chance when I found out her name wasn't Cassidy Maxwell."

She stepped forward and buried her face in his chest. She said something, her vocal cords vibrating over his skin, but he couldn't make out the words. "What?" he asked.

She pulled her face an inch away from him but kept

staring at his chest. "I never had a boyfriend. Not even for two weeks. You were supposed to be the only one. So I didn't—"

"Cassidy," he interrupted. "I meant what I said last night about keeping the past in the past. It's the best place for it. It doesn't matter anymore."

"I *want* you to know that."

"All right, then," he said, relenting. He couldn't help the warm feeling that filled his heart that Cassidy had held out hope for them. That even though she'd left him she had found no one else worthy.

He backed a step away from her and began again to unbutton her sweater, one small pearly button at a time. When he got to the bottom, he opened it to reveal not a pink lacy girly bra, but a wild hot-pink and orange striped cotton tank. He laughed. "It's good to see the old Cassidy zaniness is still there," he said. "All I have to do is peel the layers away."

He expected her to laugh, too, but she didn't, and before he could read her expression, she put her hand behind his neck, rose up on her toes and kissed him deeply.

Eric returned the kiss, inhaling her scent, breathing her into him so they tumbled onto the bed together like one person. They landed upside-down and his feet in socks pushed into the soft pillows. He removed his clothes in a minimal number of swift movements. He saw Cassidy start to pull off the striped tank and he stopped her. He bent his head and caught one of her nipples through the cotton, very gently, between his teeth.

He heard her gasp. He licked his lips and sucked, soaking the fabric around the sensitive bud.

Her fingernails dug into his bare shoulders. He pulled away, eliciting a cry of wordless protest. He undid her jeans and slid them down over her creamy legs. "I love all your little freckles," he said. "I think I'll count them from top to bottom." He pointed to her hairline. "One. Two. Three..."

"No," she said, kicking her jeans away and tossing her matching striped panties after them.

"No?" he teased. "Why? It shouldn't take me longer than an hour."

She grabbed his hand and placed it between her legs. She was hot, and wet, and this time Eric was the one to moan. "Well, if you have other ideas..."

He rolled onto his back, pulling Cassidy on top of him. She hovered inches above his erection, the heat emanating from her core making him harder and harder. He splayed his fingers over her slender hips and guided her down onto him very, very slowly until he was fully inside her.

She did nothing for a long, agonizing moment, then she began to move. She watched his face and whatever she saw there encouraged her to rock faster, rubbing, creating friction that made Eric nearly bite his own tongue.

Her eye caught something beyond him, and when she continued to gaze, he arched his neck back slightly to see what had her attention. When he realized she was watching herself in the large mirror over the dresser, he nearly lost control, but he forced himself to wait.

He'd waited so long for her, for them, already.

As Cassidy's breathing began to speed up, coming in fast pants, Eric deepened his thrusts, pushing against her and into her faster and faster until together they went over the edge into sweet, throbbing oblivion.

Eventually they righted themselves so their heads were sharing one pillow and they were underneath the covers, their skin pressed together. They weren't sleeping, just accustoming themselves to the serenity of their embrace.

"I can't believe I'm saying this," Eric said softly, "but we have to be up early to go to school tomorrow."

He thought he felt Cassidy stiffen for a moment, then relax again.

"I love you," she said.

He laid a hand on her cheek. "I love you, too," he answered, kissing her on the temple. Wispy strands of her hair caught in his mouth, but he didn't brush them away.

She pressed her palm over his hand, held it there for a moment, then wrapped her arm over his back. She held on very tight, her fingers clutching the sheet around him. She held on as though she never wanted to let go.

She held on as if she was scared.

No, Eric thought. This had to be one of those rare moments when he was interpreting Cassidy wrong.

Perhaps she just couldn't believe that this was all happening, he thought. So she's clinging to him. He could understand that. He felt it, too. Felt the relief of finally being able to love her.

She's just relieved, he decided, *and maybe a little cold. It's chilly in here.* He kissed her again and went to sleep.

As Eric drove through the main gates of the Saunders University campus, Cassidy went cold.

College campuses were designed, it seemed, to remain unchanged. Especially classic, hilly Massachusetts campuses. She remembered seeing faded black-and-white photos in the catalogs and old yearbooks of Saunders football players in what looked like dark wooly uniforms, rah-rah frat boys in letter jackets and raccoon coats, and smiling coed girls in full skirts and saddle shoes. Cassidy remembered how the faces were unfamiliar, the clothes costume-like, but she could recognize every spot on campus—the football field, the quad, the library steps.

Students moved in and out, knowledge expanded, and years passed, but the campus stayed frozen in time.

They drove on the access road past dorm buildings, three of which Cassidy had called home. She could see posters and flags for sports teams covering windows. Students milled all around, chatting, giggling, and Cassidy said in wonder, "They're so young…"

Eric grinned. "Feeling old, are you?"

"No," she said quietly. "I just forgot…how young I was."

Eric took her hand.

He found a parking space in front of one of the main brick administrative buildings. "I think I have to go secure myself some kind of parking pass," he said.

Cassidy nodded.

"Do you want to walk around a little? Get caught up in some nostalgia?"

She nodded again and Eric opened his door and got out. Cassidy found herself unable to move and was startled as Eric pulled her door open for her from the outside. He offered his hand to help her out of the car.

"You didn't have to do that," Cassidy said. "I was just dawdling."

"That's all right. I'll meet you back here in five minutes. Where did I put my wallet?" he asked himself, fumbling inside his inside coat pocket. "Here it is. Oh, and here's something else. I completely forgot about it."

He handed her an object she knew, but for a split second didn't recognize out of context. It was the Welcome cat from her door in London.

"How did you—" she started, and he explained he'd gotten it from her maintenance guy.

"I'm actually glad I forgot until now," Eric said, "because now is appropriate. Welcome back to Saunders. And allow me to do something else that's finally appropriate in front of everyone." He kissed her full on the lips and touched her nose with his. "See you in a few."

She watched him as he walked to the administration building. There was a bit of a spring in his step, one she hadn't seen since they were on this same campus together.

The last two nights were the kind she'd been dreaming pink, bubbly, lovely dreams about her whole life. She could still feel his warm embrace. In the middle of the night, the memories came back, Randall Greene threatening her again, pointing out she had more to lose than just an A in a class, but when she woke up again, became lucid, she was protected in Eric's arms. He hadn't heard her awaken and she'd studied him while he'd slept—lips slightly parted, face rough with the beginnings of stubble, his hair rumpled. Even as he was unconscious, she'd felt the safety of him.

He didn't know it, but she'd risk it all today. Because it was time. Because she had to, to live her life the real way, as the real—

"Cassidy Maxwell!"

Cassidy whirled at a woman's voice. Who was that?

She saw two people in the distance, both frantically waving at her. She held her own palm up in confused greeting, still trying to figure out who they were. They hurried over to her, and as they got closer, one called, "We'd know you ten miles away, Cassidy, from that gorgeous hair!"

As the two women got closer, Cassidy recognized her former Saunders classmates—Sandra Westport and Jane Jackson. They ran to her and hugged her in that enthusiastic way old female friends have, complete with high-pitched shrieking and frenzied hopping.

Despite her trepidation at being here again, despite her fear of the immense tasks ahead of her—or perhaps because of it, Cassidy let herself get caught up in the happy reunion.

They pulled away and Cassidy examined her old friends as they gave her the good-natured once-over, as well. Jane had been the one to comment on Cassidy's hair, which was funny because her own flaming hair would stand her out in any crowd. Her impossibly pale green eyes shone with delight. As for Sandra, well, if she'd donned her old Saunders cheerleading skirt right now and skipped out onto the football field, her blond-haired, blue-eyed looks would still fool all the fans into thinking she was still a freshman.

"We've really missed you, Cassidy," Sandra said. "We all knew you would be doing something special. The embassy! Living in London! We should all be so glamorous."

Cassidy smiled. "It's not exactly that, but—"

"Oh, just fib and tell us it is," Jane said, "so we can live vicariously through you."

"Well, then, it's just tea parties and shopping all the time," Cassidy said, laughing. "And men who all look like Hugh Grant and Austin Powers."

"Yep, I knew it," Sandra said with her all-American grin.

"It's wonderful to see you," Cassidy said. "I've been so wrapped up in—things—that I forgot some of you would be here, too."

"I'm always here," Jane said, "I work for Gilbert."

"All the male students must come in and fall all over you," Cassidy commented.

"Well, now I have a good reason to turn them away," Jane said, holding up a modest but twinkly engagement ring.

Cassidy grabbed her hand and let out the requisite squeal. "I'm so happy for you," Cassidy said.

"Me, too," Jane confessed.

"Smith Parker," Sandra said to Cassidy, winking. "I approve."

"I remember him," Cassidy said. "He was a really bright student back then. And cute, of course."

"I went through a rough divorce," Jane told Cassidy. "I have a wonderful little boy from that marriage, but when a man leaves, you think you're never going to be happy in love again. But, you know, life surprises you."

Cassidy nodded. That was certainly true. "And Sandra?" Cassidy asked with a pretense of slyness. "Still with the dashing David Westport? The man that all cheerleaders tumbled over themselves to be close to?"

"The very same," Sandra said.

"Look at her, she's got that blissed-out newlywed expression going," Jane said. "You'd never think they were ball-and-chaining it for so long."

"It's better than ever. *We're* better than ever," Sandra admitted. "And that's not just an empty expression."

As Sandra closed her eyes for a moment to savor the thought, Jane and Cassidy sighed girlish sighs of shared happiness at a fairy tale come true.

"Well, while we're on the topic," Sandra said, "are you not Cassidy *Maxwell* anymore? Are you married to a proper British fellow?"

"I've seen that Ambassador Cole on TV, by the way," Jane said. "Age difference or not, he could make a woman really get interested in current events."

Cassidy laughed. "I'm not married, and for the record, the ambassador is like my uncle," she said. She was considering whether and how to tell them about Eric, when she felt a shadow hovering over her shoulder. She saw the expressions on her old friends' faces transform from curiosity to understanding. Then she felt an arm around her shoulder.

"Girl talk?" Eric asked. "I always loved girl talk. Keep going. Don't mind me."

"Eric, you remember Sandra Westport and Jane Jackson," Cassidy said.

"Sure I do. It's nice to see you two again. You both look fabulous. These little college coeds can't compete."

Jane preened, but Sandra raised her eyebrows mockingly. "Flattery's not going to get you out of this one, Barnes," she said. "There's the small matter of the C-plus I got in poli-sci when you were my T.A."

"Um, uh..." Eric pretended to stammer.

"All right, kids," Jane said. "Let's hash it out over lunch in the student union dining hall."

Sandra punched Eric's arm lightly. "Oh, I forgive you. Especially since you seem to mean something to my old pal Cassidy. You can fill us in on all the details over a burger."

"*Is* it a burger?" Eric asked. "Or...is it mystery meat?"

"Speaking of mystery," Jane said. "There's something we need to fill you guys in on, in terms of Gilbert Harrison and all the secrets around here. I'll call Rachel on the way and tell her to meet us at the dining hall," she said to Sandra.

"Rachel James?" Cassidy asked.

"The one and the same," Sandra confirmed.

"This Gilbert situation has really created quite the little reunion," Eric commented.

Cassidy just nodded, her mind working fast.

Chapter Twelve

Lunch was like a time warp, with the four Saunders grads sliding into easy conversation over lunch. "I always did like mac-and-cheese day," Eric said, and they all agreed, spooning up the pasta happily.

Jane and Sandra pestered Eric and Cassidy for details of their new relationship, but both Eric and Cassidy hedged their answers a bit, and the two women, smart enough to know they were poking at something still too fragile to withstand scrutiny, let it go, sharing a knowing grin. Then Jane regaled them all with interesting tales of comings and goings of alumni and professors, proving she had her finger on the pulse of the school.

Cassidy was enjoying herself until Sandra said, "Remember that whole Randall Greene business?"

Jane shook her head. "Who could forget that charming jerk? What a complete pig he turned out to be."

Cassidy's fork froze halfway to her mouth.

"Wasn't he the guy who got himself mixed up with female students?" Eric asked. "I remember something about that."

"Yep," Jane confirmed. "He would have gotten away with all that stuff, too, if the media hadn't gotten wind of him somehow."

"Didn't you have him for one of your classes?" Eric asked Cassidy.

Cassidy broke out into a small sweat, then looked up and cried, "Rachel!"

Her former classmate couldn't have come a moment too soon. Cassidy had a master plan for today, and she wanted to talk about Randall Greene, and everything else, on her own terms.

Rachel approached their table with an uncharacteristically shy smile. "Hi, guys," she said. "Cassidy, how nice to see you!"

Cassidy stood to give Rachel a kiss on the cheek. Cassidy marveled at how beautiful Rachel still looked, but there was a sadness painted within the beauty of her face.

"How's everything with you?" Cassidy asked, trying to make the usually offhand question sound genuine.

"I'm hanging in there," Rachel offered. "Things have—been rough." She didn't say anything more. Cassidy, who knew a thing or two about people who wanted to keep their problems inside, didn't push. She gave

Rachel a one-armed hug as Eric pulled a chair away from another table for the new arrival.

"Well, now that we're all here," Sandra said, "I think it's time to let Cassidy in on a little secret. Eric, since you were good enough to cross an ocean to bring our Cassidy home, I think you deserve to hear this, too. Many generous things have been done for the benefit of several students, including several unethical things like grade-changing. These have been traced to Gilbert, who's claimed that he's been acting on behalf of a mysterious, rich benefactor."

"We have heard that," Eric said. Cassidy nodded assent.

"Yes, well," Jane said, "Jacob Weber and Ella Gardner—who are now a couple, by the way—have informed a very small group of us of the identity of this benefactor."

Cassidy leaned forward.

"It's Gilbert," Jane said. "Gilbert himself."

Cassidy's hand flew to her chest, lying flat over her heart. "What?"

"He inherited the money from his grandfather," Sandra said.

"Are they sure?" Eric asked, and Cassidy could feel her heart beginning to thump hard, pushing against her palm.

"They were sure, but Sandra and Rachel and I have done a little...unofficial digging around," Jane said. "We've found documentation. It's true."

Cassidy's mind was spinning. Gilbert himself? Gilbert had— She couldn't believe it. It was one thing to think that her old professor had been using his influence to help students, but he'd actually been using his own money, his own connections? Cassidy didn't know why he'd been compelled to do this for students, or how he chose the beneficiaries. Her chest filled with gratefulness for him with what she was now certain he must have done for her, and her heart filled with guilt at keeping her distance when she learned his truth. He'd come through for her when she needed help, but she hadn't been there for him, even just to be his friend. She'd been going through her own hell, but still, she felt sorry.

Luckily, she had already planned to put it right today.

"Cassidy," Sandra said, "we also know enough about Gilbert now to know he's hiding something else. Something big. But we can't figure out what it is."

"You were his work-study student, in his office, back when we were at school," Jane added. "Can you tell us anything? Anything he might have told you? Anything you accidentally came across?"

Cassidy glanced at each woman in turn, eyeing Rachel last. She hadn't said much, but she was also casting a hopeful expression at Cassidy.

Cassidy didn't answer for a long time, weighing her words carefully. Everyone at the table, still accustomed to Cassidy's deliberate reticence, waited with patience for her response.

"No, I can't tell you anything," Cassidy finally said honestly. "I'm sorry."

The three women let out a collective breath of disappointment. "It's still a conundrum," Sandra said. "I mean, I'm willing to stand up for Gilbert no matter what, but it would be easier if I knew his whole situation."

"I think—maybe I can at least offer some advice," Cassidy said.

"What's that?" Jane asked.

"Perhaps you should try to talk to him," Cassidy said. "As friends. Gently. Just…ask him. If you believe he has something to hide, maybe giving him the opportunity to unburden himself to people who care about him will bring it out in an honest way."

They nodded slowly, mulling her words.

Eric wrapped an arm around Cassidy's shoulder and whispered into her ear, "How did you get so wise?"

She leaned into his heat, seeking the comfort she needed. "I couldn't help it," she murmured. "I had a good teacher."

Eric and Cassidy waved goodbye to their old friends on the quad, all of them promising to get together one night before the end of the week. Then Cassidy turned to Eric. Her courage had been MIA for the past decade. Now that she'd found it, she wasn't going to let it slip away again.

"I need to see Gilbert Harrison now," she told Eric. "I'm going to his office."

"Great idea," he said. "I've been looking forward to it. I didn't tell him you'd finally decided to come, so I can't wait to see the look on his face when you walk in."

"Eric," Cassidy said, taking his hand. "Listen."

Eric stilled, searching her face. "What's wrong?"

"Nothing. It's just—" She stared at a fixed point next to his ear, trying to decide how to translate her feelings.

"You're not the only person I left things badly with when I was done at Saunders. I was crummiest to you, but I also left some…unfinished business with Gilbert, and I feel awful about it because it appears he never stopped being a good friend to me."

Eric stroked her cheek.

"I really would like to see him alone for a few minutes," Cassidy added. "There are some things I want to say to—apologize. Put things right."

"Of course." Eric kissed the top of her head. "I understand."

Hang on to that understanding, Cassidy begged silently. *You're going to need much more of it. Later.*

"I'll run to the library to check my e-mail," Eric said. "Then I'll come by when I'm done. Will that be enough time?"

"Yes. Thank you. Does he have the same office?"

"What do you think? Do you remember where it is?"

"I remember everything," Cassidy said. "Even though I tried not to, deep down I did remember everything."

Eric's face creased with puzzlement. "I'm not sure I get what you mean."

She kissed his lips and felt him smile under her touch. "Good luck," he said. "See you later."

Cassidy ascended one flight of stairs heavily and slowly, then walked down a short hallway, getting reaccustomed to the smell of the brick building, the smell of dusty papers and books, the sound of clicking computer keyboards and whirring copy machines.

Her heart beat a little faster when she reached Gilbert Harrison's office, but she reminded herself that Gilbert's heart would probably speed up, as well, upon seeing her, and she would have to be the strong one. The wise one.

The door was the same. The paint was peeling a little more, but the same. She knocked without hesitation.

"Come in!" she heard her old professor call.

She took a deep breath and entered.

Gilbert was seated in that same saggy leather chair that Cassidy remembered, the one he let her sit in to read chapters or to outline a paper, when her filing work for him was finished.

He rose to his feet and Cassidy noticed he had nothing in his hands—no papers to grade, no textbook. It was as if he'd just been sitting there, waiting for her, waiting for something to happen to him. She wondered how many days he'd been sitting and waiting, doing nothing. She wanted to cry for him. Instead she put out her hand.

"Professor," Cassidy said. "It's wonderful to see you."

He approached her and took her hand in that tentative way men have with women, but years of politicking with the ambassador had taught Cassidy how to shake hands for real. She could see it surprised him.

"Cassidy Maxwell," he finally said, mustering a weak smile. "If I hadn't already heard how successful you were, I'd know it by that grip." He gestured to the office behind him. "Please, come in. Have a seat."

Cassidy fell into the old stuffed chair. The leather squeaked underneath her jeans, and she tucked her feet underneath her, like she used to. She knew Gilbert wouldn't ask her to keep her shoes off the chair. He never had.

Gilbert sat across from her in his desk chair, but there wasn't much space between them. His office was as cramped as ever, with books spilling off his shelves and manila folders in precarious piles all over his desk.

"Some things never change," Cassidy offered.

Gilbert shook his head sadly. "I wish some things didn't."

His once-dark hair had a lot of gray and Cassidy wondered how much of it had been gradual and how much had happened with the pain of the past semester.

Half hidden behind a stack of papers on his desk, Cassidy saw the framed picture of his wife, the one Cassidy remembered.

"I'm very, very sorry about your wife," Cassidy said. "I only just heard."

Gilbert nodded, a shadow passing over his face. But he kept his gaze on Cassidy and his hands twisted together in his lap.

Cassidy didn't want her friend to worry longer than he had to. She was ready to say what she came here to say.

"I've had a hard time," she said. "I've made some very wrong decisions, and I chose to suffer in secret for many years."

Gilbert's eyebrows pushed together nearly an inch, but he continued to listen.

"I threw away my best opportunity for happiness. I love my job, I'm living in the most wonderful city in the world, but I knew what I was missing. I trained myself not to think about what I did and what I lost. I refused to give in to the emotion, so that I could at least live my life. But no matter what I did, it hurt. It hurt every single day."

Gilbert's face was filled with empathy, as Cassidy was sure it would be.

"Then Eric turned up in London and found me," she said, "and I was forced to look into the face of what I'd lost, of who I'd lost. I tried to resist it, wait it out until he went away again. But he stayed. And then, Gilbert, it was the strangest thing— It was as if messages kept coming to me, blinking at me, obvious messages that I couldn't ignore."

"What do you mean?" Gilbert asked.

Cassidy shook her head. She'd planned to explain this today to Gilbert but she still didn't know quite how. "There was a bombing—I thought for a few minutes that Eric had been killed, or injured. It told me that life is short, that… And then, I made a friend. She wasn't… around for very long, but it was as if she was in my life just long enough to teach me that you can't keep secrets from the people you love. That you can only have the fullness of their love if they know the honest, real you. Then I met a stranger, a man I never met before and probably will never see again. But he saw through me and he warned me not to let fear take over. He told me to be strong."

Cassidy stopped, shaking her head. "Just in the past two weeks, all of this."

Neither she nor Gilbert said anything for a while, both swimming in the seas of their own thoughts.

"In the context of a personal conversation," Gilbert eventually said, "that's the most I ever heard you say at one time."

The corners of her mouth twitched up. "I didn't tell you the last thing. Ambassador Cole told me yesterday that there are no failures, just trip-ups on the way to setting things right. Then I thought, my God, my last ten years have been one very long trip-up."

"Cassidy," Gilbert said softly. "I remember when you used to bounce in here, your ponytail flopping, a big grin on your face, to tell me about something you learned in class, something that excited you, something you wanted me to talk about with you some more. Full of questions, always, and you wanted answers. I did my best for you then. But I don't know what you want me to do for you now."

"I am telling you what I learned," Cassidy said. "I learned that secrets can destroy a person. If someone else finds out and exposes you, well, that's bad, but it's even worse to keep it locked away forever. In your mind. In a safe. You'll lose the happiness you could have."

Gilbert blinked, but otherwise his gaze held steady.

She let that sink in a moment, then continued, "You see, I'm about to set my own things right by telling the truth. It's a huge risk. It may mean I lose the greatest thing I have, but still, I'm convinced now that the truth is freeing. And I'm telling you this because I have this little feeling it might free you, too."

Gilbert did nothing for a full minute. Then he nodded.

She stood. "I'll be speaking to Mr. Broadstreet on your behalf, and I'll be happy to do it."

"Thank you," he said. He put out his hand again, but Cassidy hugged him instead. She could tell he was surprised, but he patted his hands on her back.

"No," she said quietly, hugging him even more tightly. "Thank you. Thank you." *For everything,* she added silently.

There was a light rap on the door and Cassidy pulled away from the professor, wiping at her eyes. Eric and Gilbert shook hands, then Eric put an arm around Cassidy. She loved how he did that so casually, and so often. It was beneficial, too, to close the space between them. Only two people could fit comfortably in this office.

"Were you surprised to see her?" Eric asked their old professor.

"Believe me, I couldn't have been happier."

"Then it was worth what I went through to drag her back," Eric joked, and Cassidy gave him a good-natured elbow to the ribs.

Then Eric grew sober. "It's not fair what you're going through," he said. "It's not right. But everything will work out. We're all here now and we're all behind you one hundred percent."

Cassidy nodded in agreement.

Gilbert eyed them, and asked, "Together again, I see?"

Cassidy felt herself blush. Eric gave her a squeeze.

"Well," Gilbert said, "then at least something good came out of my predicament."

"It will all turn out good," Eric assured him. "Try not to worry. I'll drop by and say hi tomorrow, all right?"

They all said goodbye and Eric led Cassidy from the room. Before Gilbert closed the door, she peered over her shoulder at him. He winked at her and she returned it.

As Cassidy and Eric left his office, Gilbert wondered if it signified the end of your career as an educator when your student returned to teach you a lesson.

She'd said she was about to put things right. Gilbert had a suspicion it had something to do with Eric. He hoped Eric had retained the sensibility he'd shown as a young adult. That when Cassidy dished out her hurt, Eric could swallow it and move on.

Meanwhile, Gilbert resettled himself on his leather chair. Cassidy had not only insinuated that she wasn't interested in exposing his truths, but she'd subtly suggested that perhaps it was time that Gilbert spill his secret himself.

Was he ready to do that? After all this time? Were the people that would be affected ready to hear it?

He leaned his head against the cracked leather and closed his eyes. He had a hunch he'd be sitting here, mulling it over, until late into the night. He also had a feeling that by the time morning came, he still wouldn't have the answers.

"I have to talk to you about something," Cassidy said as they walked away from the brick building.

"Sure, what?"

"Can we find a quiet spot?"

"Why don't we just talk about it in the car on the way back to the hotel?" Eric suggested. "I have to make a few phone calls this afternoon if I want to stay away from work a few more days. Then we can relax until dinner. Nap or watch TV, or something else, if you prefer."

He bent to kiss her cheek, but Cassidy was shaking her head even before he got out the last word. "No, I want to tell you here."

"Um, all right. How about back here somewhere?" They began to walk around the side of the building when they heard, "Excuse me."

They turned and found a man hurrying toward them. He pulled a slim reporter's-style notebook out of his back pocket and Cassidy scowled.

"I'm Ian Beck," he said, and named the national newspaper for which he worked. "And you are?"

"Busy," Eric said, tugging gently on Cassidy's sleeve.

"Are you students, or former students, of Gilbert Harrison?"

"You're here for Gilbert?" Eric asked in spite of himself.

"Yes. May I ask you a few questions?"

Cassidy felt Eric take in the sort of breath one fortified oneself with before entering into a tirade. She stopped him with a hand on his shoulder. She would handle this. She spent half her career dealing with the press.

"We have no comment," Cassidy said.

The reporter opened his mouth and Cassidy interrupted him before he could begin. "If you change your mind and perhaps decide to write a decent, intelligent story that holds actual importance for thousands and thousands of people, such as the Northern Ireland conflict, I'd be happy to arrange an interview with you. Regarding Gilbert Harrison and the fish-wrap copy I imagine you'll write about him, however, don't expect my help."

"Yes, ma'am," the reporter said with a good-natured smile. Eric and Cassidy turned away from him.

"Good work," Eric said. "But I suspect we haven't seen the last of him. Still want to talk?"

"Yes. I have to." Cassidy was almost grateful for the unexpected blindside by the reporter. It removed her one step from her emotions, for the moment. Enough to start what she had to finish.

Eric led her around the side of the building, where they found a small wooden bench facing the periphery of the campus. There was no path there, so no students were likely to round the corner and see them. It was a bit warm for midautumn, but the bench was cool underneath Cassidy when she sat. She pulled her knees up to her chest and leaned against the armrest so she could see Eric as she spoke.

She cleared her throat, which felt fuzzy and thick. She tried to be still and to feel Sophie's presence in the air around her, encouraging her the way Cassidy knew she would have, had she ever had the chance to return to London.

Eric looked at her and Cassidy memorized his face the way it was now. The way she might never see it again after this conversation. The way she might always have to just remember it.

"I want to tell you why I stood you up on graduation day," Cassidy said, and was surprised at herself, at the calm, even tone that emerged from within her.

"I don't want you to," Eric said. "I already told you. It's in the past. It doesn't matter to what we are now."

"But it does," Cassidy said. "I love you."

"I love you, too."

"You love the me you know. But there's a bit of me you don't know. If we're going to love each other, go into the future together, I can't keep this from you any longer. I want you to know everything."

Eric opened his mouth to speak, but Cassidy covered it with her hand. "Let me get it all out," she whispered. "Or I might not. And I have to."

Eric kissed her palm and Cassidy nearly broke down and wept at the tenderness she literally held in her hand. She took it away and hugged her knees. Then she spoke again.

"Two months before graduation, I had to get my wisdom teeth out. I ignored the pain for so long, but I couldn't anymore. I was in agony. So I did it. I thought it would be one day of recovery, then nothing. But they took all four out at once. I was in terrible shape. I couldn't get out of bed."

"I remember that. I wanted to take care of you—" Eric began, then said, "Sorry. Go on."

"I know you wanted to take care of me," Cassidy said. "But I was young, I was vain, I didn't want you to see me with my face a mess. I couldn't eat more than soup for days. I couldn't sleep for the soreness and pain. And one thing I absolutely could not do was study. And that was horrible to me, because I'd taken on all these extra honors projects and had to prepare for several on-campus job recruitments. I fell behind. I just fell way behind.

"There was one class I had one last paper due in. I didn't even read half of what I needed to read, and I'd missed a bunch of classes by that time. I wasn't even afraid of failing, I was afraid of getting less than an A. It sounds silly now, but it was my world then. You know that. I had to get the paper done on time, and it had to be good. So I did something I've regretted ever since. I—I plagiarized. I plagiarized it."

Eric felt his mouth fall open. He looked at the brightest, smartest woman he'd ever known and was shocked.

"I never did it before, ever," Cassidy insisted. "I never cheated on so much as a spelling test. But ironically, that turned out to be a bad thing. Because I was a novice at cheating, I got caught. The professor smoked me right out.

"He threatened to tell the administration. I would have been thrown out, Eric. I never would have earned my diploma, after everything I had worked for. But then, he offered me a way out." She stopped and swallowed hard. Eric's mind was already spinning. He couldn't imagine what was coming next, but he predicted the plagiarism, bad as it was, wasn't the worst part of this story.

"I told him I'd think about it. I went back to my dorm

room and sat there on the floor, in the dark, for hours. I wanted so much to call you, to ask for your help. But I knew how you felt about plagiarism. We both had scholarships. And I'd remembered you saying once that when anyone at Saunders plagiarized, it personally offended you, because people like us had to work hard to be there, and someone cheating was an extra slap in the face. And I agreed with you. And I still did, even after doing it myself. You would have been so angry, and you would have been right. I couldn't tell you. I couldn't tell anyone. I was so alone."

Eric watched as she brought her shaking hands up to her face, covering it for a very brief moment before she dropped them onto her knees and continued.

"Accepting this professor's solution was the only way out," she said. "But I could hardly bear it. I had these painkillers, these pills the oral surgeon gave me. I thought about the numb, warm haze they'd put me in the week before when I was laid up, and I took a couple right then and there. Then I took two more. Then I went to the professor's house."

"His house?" Eric asked. "His house? At night?"

"Eric," she said. "It was Professor Greene." She paused. "Professor Randall Greene."

Chapter Thirteen

Randall Greene? Randall Greene. Eric's blood froze in his veins. Greene was the one who—

Mixed up with female students.

No. Absolutely not. He had to be understanding this all wrong.

"I slept with him," Cassidy said, her words like a slap in the face. "That was the deal he offered me. If I slept with him, he wouldn't rat me out and destroy my academic record."

Eric instinctively put his hands over his ears to block what he was hearing, but he couldn't block the image of Cassidy, his innocent Cassidy who'd touched no one but him her whole life, undressing and lying down and moving her naked body—

Cassidy's fingers were on his skin as she tried to remove his hands from his head, but he recoiled, pulling himself out of her reach as if she'd burned him. "Don't touch me," he commanded. "Just do not touch me."

Cassidy obeyed. She straightened her legs in front of her, not looking at him anymore. "How could I have told you that? The whole reason we weren't together yet was—"

"Because I was a teacher," Eric said. His back teeth ground together hard. His clenched jaw hurt.

"I'd wanted my whole life to be with no one but you. But he threatened me," she repeated. "I didn't know what else to do. And it turned out to not even matter."

"How could it have not mattered?" he demanded.

"Because he flunked me anyway. He didn't get me thrown out of school, but he gave me an F. I cornered him after that last class and begged him to tell me why. He said it was because I'd refused to stay the night."

Eric shook his head, trying to clear away the nightmare in front of him.

"After I did it…it was—it was just that one time—I went home and took a two-hour shower. I got into bed and didn't get up for days. Then I tried to finish my classes. I really honestly tried, but I was so far gone by then. I dragged myself through every day, under the weight of the painkillers I was taking like candy. I got my family doctor, the oral surgeon and the campus clinic to all give me prescriptions. None of them knew about the others. Sadly, it was pretty easy to do. I tried to block everything out, but every difficult moment of my life felt like a consequence of what I had done. I flunked a couple of other classes—I just couldn't finish the requirements. And I stayed away from you. I couldn't face you."

"I saw you," Eric said without emotion. "In the library that one time."

"I had to get away from you," Cassidy said, her voice trembling. "Of all the stupid mistakes I had made, I was so sure the worst one would have been letting you see what I had become, telling you everything I did. I couldn't bear to have you reject me. You were everything to me, for as long as I could remember. I couldn't bear for you to leave me. So—I left you."

In Eric's raw and vulnerable state of mind, the last of those three memories—the ones he never let himself remember—rushed in, plunged in like a knife in his heart.

He was standing under the tree at noon, the one under which they'd decided to begin their new life as a couple. He watched the graduates parade around, identical clones in black robes of accomplishment, but he was certain he'd immediately recognize her by her hair, from her electric smile, from the way she would glide among her classmates.

He searched all the faces, worried, then told himself that perhaps she was planning some kind of little surprise. She was like that. He had one for her, too. He put his hand in his pocket and fingered the etched gold of the locket he was going to give her. Inside was their picture. A picture of them smiling together the night of her

Sweet Sixteen party. The night she'd kissed him. The night he'd realized she'd spoiled him for anyone else forever.

He grew hot underneath his ironed shirt and best tie. "Have you seen Cassidy Maxwell?" he began to ask the faces that floated past. "Have you seen Cassidy?"

Everyone knew Cassidy. But no one knew where she was.

He refused to move from his spot. What if she arrived and he wasn't here? Then she would think he changed his mind. She'd leave, dejected and alone.

At ten o'clock at night, Eric was still there. Collapsed at the base of the tree trunk, fingernails adding his own frustrated scratches to the artistic ones on the locket.

"Have you seen Cassidy Maxwell?" he asked nobody, his voice echoing across the deserted quad. Then he screamed, digging his fingers into the ground, clutching handfuls of grass. "Cassidy!"

The silence that followed the desperate uttering of her name stretched out, never ending. The woman who'd opened the door to his heart had kicked it shut. For eternity.

Or ten years. Whichever came first.

"I didn't go to graduation," Cassidy said needlessly. She twisted her torso to face him again, but he just stared at nothing over her right shoulder. "I still graduated, because I was so far ahead and had taken so many classes that I had plenty of credits to graduate. But I didn't even go to get my degree. I couldn't. I made up something for my parents, that I was sick or something. I'd moved out a week before into a little apartment off campus. It was a few towns away, a rundown neighborhood. Awful. I got a job as a waitress in the kind of truck-stop diner I was sure you wouldn't ever go to. But for the first month, every man that came in looked like you…"

Her sentence drifted off, then she started again. "It was like that every day. Work, go home, sleep, pop pills. Then one morning, with my cup of free coffee, I opened the paper and saw Randall Greene's face. The media had found him out somehow. I wasn't the only student he'd—there were others, and I read that grades were restored. I didn't want to come forward and confess that I was one of them, but a few days later, out of curiosity, I called and obtained a copy of my transcript. Not only was my grade in his class restored to what it was before the plagiarized paper, but the other classes I'd failed were brought up to passing. I didn't know how that could have happened. I thought someone had guessed, or maybe made a fortunate error in my favor."

His mind took in her sentences, processed them, like a machine on autopilot.

"I started laying off the pills a little bit," she said, "because they kept me from thinking straight, and suddenly I really wanted to think about my future again. Then I got a phone call. Out of nowhere. Recruiting me for the embassy. I interviewed and got the job right away. Before I left, a woman showed up at my door. She was a drug counselor. She offered to quietly help me. By then, I was ready to let her.

"I did wonder about my streak of good fortune. Of course, now I know. It was Gilbert, the benefactor. He somehow figured it out. I wasn't talking to him anymore. I quit my job with him after my tooth thing. I was uncomfortable around him because I was disappointed in him about something I'd found out about him. I'm sure I could've gotten over it. It had nothing to do with me. But then I brought my own problems upon myself. And I didn't want him to be disappointed in me.

"Anyhow, back then I didn't know it was Gilbert. And by the time my bags were packed and I was halfway across the Atlantic, I vowed never to think about Saunders, or Massachusetts, ever again. I was given another chance at a new life. I took it and I didn't look back."

Cassidy took a deep, shuddering breath.

"But you, Eric, *you* were the only thing I couldn't forget. I had to sacrifice us and it almost killed me. I've never touched another man since then, not ever, until you. And now that you're here again and we are what we are—"

"We're not anything," Eric informed her.

Her face crumpled slowly in front of him, and his anger at her was displaced for a moment as he realized he'd done it, that he'd badly hurt the girl he'd spent half his life trying to please and protect. But the moment was short, replaced quickly with his fresh memories of lying in bed night after night, wondering why she'd left, wondering what he'd missed, what he'd done. But she'd done it all. She'd destroyed them. "We're not anything," he said again.

"I knew I had to give you the chance to say that," Cassidy conceded, beginning to sob. "I owed you the truth. I owed *me* to reveal the truth. There it is. You know all of me."

She was crying openly, tears flowing down her exquisite face.

His chest ached within its new hollowness. He watched her cry, because he couldn't, and she had to do it for both of them.

When her sobs subsided a little bit, and she began to try to take big gasping breaths, Eric said, "I have to go. Goodbye."

He stood on cramped, shaky legs and walked away from the bench, walked away from her.

Part of him expected her to call him back. The other part of him wasn't surprised when she didn't.

Time stopped for Cassidy on the bench. She didn't know how long she sat there, alone. It was a long time, but not as long as she'd be alone in the future.

When she stood, her behind was numb and her shoulders ached with hours of defeated slouching. But her two feet were in working order. And there was one thing left to do.

Then, after testifying for Gilbert, she would return to London and start over again.

She checked her watch: 4:45. She forced herself into a jog to get halfway across campus in under five minutes.

She slipped into one of the main administration buildings, looked at the wall directory and trudged up three floors.

This office was small, quiet, unbusy. No phones were ringing. No conversation was floating around. No real reason to stay open until exactly five, but here it was, open.

Cassidy approached the small counter. The one woman there was about her mother's age and was bent over near the floor, filing. She didn't glance up until Cassidy politely cleared her throat.

"I'm sorry, dear." The woman straightened and hurried over to her. "Can I help you?"

"Yes," Cassidy said. Her voice was hoarse and her throat was raw from so much talking. And so much crying. She refused to break down again. Not now. "I'm here to pick up my degree, please."

"Of course." The woman headed back to the files again. "When did you graduate? Last spring?"

Cassidy shook her head, and told her the year.

The woman halted in her tracks. "*What* year?"

Cassidy knew the woman didn't mishear, but she repeated it anyway.

"You're running kind of late, aren't you?" the woman asked with a chuckle.

Cassidy looked her in the eye across the distance between them. "My education was incomplete," she said slowly. "But now, I've finished all my obligations. Today is my real graduation day."

She swallowed hard.

The woman's expression had transformed from amiable to sympathetic and worried. "Are you okay, dear?"

"Yes. I'd just like my degree, please."

"I have to search in the archive files to find this one. What's your name?"

"Cassidy Maxwell."

The woman disappeared and Cassidy stood very still. She stared at the countertop, afraid that if she glanced around the room, something—the color of a chair, the weave of the carpet, a picture on the wall—would give her a reason to cry again.

She did eventually check the clock, which had ticked past five. After some time, the woman returned with an oversize envelope. "Well, you're in luck." She slid the thick, creamy paper from the envelope and held it up.

Cassidy saw the Saunders University emblem, the raised gold seal, the college president's signature, and her own name in elaborate, old-fashioned, nearly unrecognizable type. She ran a finger over it. Her eyes welled up again. She stared up at the fluorescent light for a moment to drive the tears back, then she said, "Thank you."

The woman slid the degree back into the envelope and taped it shut.

"I'm sorry to keep you," Cassidy said.

"Don't be silly. You know what? This was the best part of my day."

Cassidy held out her right hand for the envelope, but the woman shook her head with a kind smile. She grasped Cassidy's outstretched hand and shook it, passing the envelope between their left hands.

"I think you need to do this right," the woman said. "Congratulations, Ms. Maxwell."

Eric jammed his hands into his coat pockets as he walked. He was just walking. He'd had to remove himself from the Saunders campus, get away from the site where he got his heart broken twice. By the same woman.

His mind was racing from one thought to the next, and his body, trying to keep up with the mental pace, moved manically, aimlessly, around the streets surrounding the campus.

Plagiarizing? He remembered the bright-eyed, young, freshman Cassidy, stumbling up the stairs with her boom box inside a laundry basket. "We're neighbors again," she'd said…

Eric turned abruptly right down a quiet street.

Randall Greene? But Eric remembered Cassidy had touched Eric's hand once, and the electrical jolt had affected them both, and they agreed they'd made the right decision, to wait until she'd graduated before moving on, to wait until it was appropriate.

Eric crossed the street and turned left again.

Drugs? He remembered Cassidy stretched out on her narrow dorm bed, trying to study with a splitting headache, waving away the ibuprofen he'd brought her, saying it made her feel fuzzy and she had to work.

Eric turned an about-face and kept walking.

He was mad at Cassidy. Was he mad? Well, the present Cassidy, the adult Cassidy, had not made the mistakes. The past Cassidy, the kid Cassidy, had. But could you be angry at a kid who made such terrible mistakes and regretted them so deeply?

He just *was* angry. He couldn't let go. He didn't want to let go of the betrayal.

She had told him her story, piling shocker upon shocker as he'd sat there, disbelieving. But that was how it had happened to her. The drug abuse was to forget the pain of sleeping with the professor. The sleeping with the professor was her chosen consequence of plagiarizing a paper.

Eric wasn't a fool, though. He'd been a teacher himself. Randall Greene had been the one in power. He'd taken advantage of Cassidy. She'd consented, but he'd deliberately put her in a no-other-way-out position.

He had a flash of harder rage then. He wanted to find Randall Greene and make him pay. That, however, wasn't the issue anymore. Greene had paid. Not enough, but he had been exposed, fired and humiliated.

The only real, deliberate mistake that Cassidy had made was plagiarizing a paper. And how much of even that was only her fault? Academically, she'd driven herself hard, and no one—not her parents, not her friends, not him—had stopped her at any point to tell her that straight A's were not everything. Damn, he himself had even encouraged her to study harder, to out-debate him, to best him. She very often did.

At what cost?

Eric made another random left, taking him past a long block of small businesses.

One big spiral. The starting point? A toothache. Her wisdom teeth.

Wisdom teeth.

He could feel a thought forming, an idea about wisdom teeth and the irony of it all—

Then he idly glanced into a storefront window and stopped short, nearly tripping over his own feet.

There, in a corner. Surrounded by pawn shop treasures—music boxes, antique cameos, yellowed baby shoes. It was there in the corner. A tooth.

Eric rubbed his eyes, certain he'd now officially gone insane. But when he looked again, it was still there.

He yanked open the pawn shop door, the bell jangle startling the elderly man behind the glass counter.

"What is that little thing in the corner of the window?" Eric demanded. "The thing that looks like a tooth."

"You'll have to show me," the man said. He rose from his stool, hitched up his worn navy pants and accompanied Eric to the window. He followed the younger man's pointing finger.

"Oh, yeah. I'm not sure," the shop owner admitted. "Guy brought it in the other day in a box of junk. Said it was a shark's tooth." He shrugged. "Can't verify that, but it's kind of interesting, so hey, I threw it in the window."

"I want it," Eric said.

"Sure." The man reached over and plucked it out of the window.

"I have something to trade," Eric said.

He slipped his hand into the front pocket of his jeans and pulled out the etched locket. The one he'd intended to give Cassidy ten years ago, under the tree.

When he was packing to go to London, he'd tossed it into his suitcase. He hadn't known why at the time. He didn't think it was out of hope that he'd actually be able to give it to her. It was more like a talisman. Or kind of like when you gave a search dog a piece of someone's clothing to sniff him out. Having the locket in his suitcase just seemed to be the right thing to do to add a little luck to finding Cassidy.

This morning, he'd checked the suitcase pocket for clean socks and discovered it. Smiling to himself, he'd slipped it into his pants' pocket, figuring maybe he'd have a moment on the Saunders campus to give it to her.

Then she'd dropped her bomb on his romantic scenario.

Or maybe…maybe he'd dropped it on her scenario. A scenario of redemption.

He opened the locket and pulled out the picture inside of Cassidy Maxwell and Eric Barnes, two young people who were gone now, except for memories.

He threw the locket on the counter.

The man picked it up, opened it, ran his fingers over it, and looked sternly at Eric. "Much as I like the opportunity to seal a deal in my favor," he said, "you can't call this an even trade. This is a 14-carat gold locket. That's just a piece of junk, really."

"That's all right," Eric said, getting excited. "It's fine."

"It's not an even trade," the man repeated. "That tooth doesn't have nearly the worth of this locket."

"Believe me," Eric said, "it does."

Chapter Fourteen

Eric sprinted back to the campus. It had grown dark, and students went from dining halls to dorms to library stacks, enjoying the part of school that wasn't really school, but their current way of life.

He sought out the bench Cassidy had been on when he'd left her. But now it was occupied by a young couple, kissing passionately, notebooks on the ground next to their feet.

He walked all around the campus, peering around buildings and behind trees. He ended up at the parked rental car. It had gotten colder and he turned up his collar against the increasing wind.

He navigated the car back to the motel in closest walking distance. He asked for Cassidy at the front desk, and when it was determined that she was not a guest there, he got himself a room. He unloaded his bag and Cassidy's bag onto one bed. He sat on the other, pulled out his cell phone and the nightstand Yellow Pages, and called every motel within a few miles. Cassidy hadn't checked in anywhere.

Well, she wasn't leaving the area. He was sure that regardless of what happened between them on the bench, she still planned to stay and testify for Gilbert Harrison. If he had to, he'd show up at every hearing until he found her.

But he didn't want to wait a day, two days, a week. He had to find her tonight.

He called her parents. And his parents. He dodged curious questions from all of them about what was happening. He'd fill them in when *he* knew. But in the meantime, none of them had heard from Cassidy.

He wasn't worried about her safety. Cassidy had the ability to find herself a place for the night. Maybe she'd called Sandra or Jane.

He just wanted to see her. *Had* to talk to her.

He turned on the TV, turned it off, turned it on again. He paced. He looked out the window at the empty street. He could see the wide hedges around part of the perimeter of Saunders, stripped almost bare by autumn's chill.

He was about to give up, to take a shower and go to bed, to try again in the morning. He opened his suitcase and there, on top, was the Saunders sweatshirt. The shirt he had lent Cassidy, like one he'd remembered her wearing underneath their tree once.

He slid his feet into his still-tied sneakers and sprinted out the door. One last look.

She was there.

She was sitting in the sparse grass under the tree. It was after midnight, but she was there, staring straight ahead at nothing, expressionless.

Eric stepped out of the shadows and Cassidy saw him. But her expression still didn't evolve into anything emotional.

"I want to give you something," Eric said.

Cassidy raised her brow, then lowered it. "Right. My suitcase, I assume. All right. I'm checking in somewhere later. You can just toss it over here, then."

"First, I want to talk."

"I have nothing left to say."

"I guessed as much. You certainly said a lot today."

He crouched next to her, then sat all the way down, facing her. There was a large manila envelope in her lap.

"When you told me your story today," Eric said, "my first thought was that you betrayed me. That's why I walked away. I felt like you betrayed me by becoming someone else behind my back.

"But I realized later, while walking around in circles, that the person you betrayed was yourself. You let your fear of losing me rule you. You couldn't tell me what you were going through, which just got you deeper and deeper.

"I take some blame there. You had reasons you couldn't tell me. You thought I would judge you. But you weren't a talker to anyone else. You communicated with me on a different level. And so I should never have been someone you considered closed-off, on any topic."

She was shaking her head, but he stopped her. "Let me get it all out," he said in an echo of her own plea earlier that day. "You're now standing on your own. The betrayal is over. You're moving ahead.

"I'm sorry," he blurted. "This is not coming out the way I intended. All the things I wanted to say to you are sort of tumbling around in my brain and mixing up. So, here." He handed her the small, battered box, the only gift box the man in the pawn shop could find.

Cassidy looked at the box for a long moment, then opened it up and pulled out the tooth. She held it in her hand, studied it. Then she looked up again at Eric.

"All your troubles started with your wisdom teeth," Eric said. "But you can look at it another way."

He took the tooth from her and unwound a black silk cord from the box. The shopkeeper had seen the hole in the tooth and insisted Eric at least take the silk cord as part of the trade.

Eric hung the tooth around Cassidy's neck and placed it again in her hand. He closed her hand around it and held her fist in his. "You can look at it this way," he continued. "You've arrived here, today, as Cassidy Maxwell, capable adult, successful in her career, smart and savvy. You are the culmination of the wisdom you've achieved since losing those teeth. And now you've passed some of that wisdom to me, too."

Tears began to drip down Cassidy's face. This time,

he wiped them away. "I want us to keep creating our futures together, keep gaining wisdom together, keep growing up together," he said. "I love you."

"I've loved you all my life," Cassidy whispered. "Even when you weren't in it."

"I'll never disappear from it again."

Their lips met and their sighs of relief and joy melted into each other's mouths. They grabbed at each other with the knowing that they didn't have to, that they weren't going to be torn apart ever again.

The half-moon slipped out from behind a cloud, illuminating their smiles. "I think it's time I get you into bed," Eric whispered, and Cassidy nodded. They pulled each other to their feet. "What's in the envelope?"

She handed it to him with a proud smile. "My degree."

He hugged her and said into her hair, "You worked hard for it." He pulled away to grin. "And speaking of work, don't think our reconciliation means you have to move back here. The ambassador offered to pull a few strings for me. I'm not going to turn down help from high places. And I thought London was great. Anyplace with you in it is great."

Cassidy hugged him. "Thank you," she said.

As Eric began walking to the car, Cassidy stopped. She closed her eyes, smelled the air of the place she'd hidden from, had tried to forget, and realized she never could.

"Is everything okay?" she heard him say. She opened her eyes. Eric had turned around and was watching her, concerned. "Are you feeling…all right again?"

Cassidy mentally scanned herself, every physical

sensation, from head to feet. She was different somehow. But she couldn't tell exactly how.

She stayed still. She knew Eric would wait until she was ready to answer. She was feeling—

"I feel—light," she said. Then she laughed. A weightless, free laugh of wonder. "I can't believe it. So—light!"

The man she loved smiled at her.

"I feel light," she repeated.

She unbuttoned her coat and shrugged it to the ground. She opened her arms wide, embracing everything for one moment.

Then she leaped, launched herself into the air, and turned a perfect cartwheel, her toes pointing straight up to the sky.

* * * * *

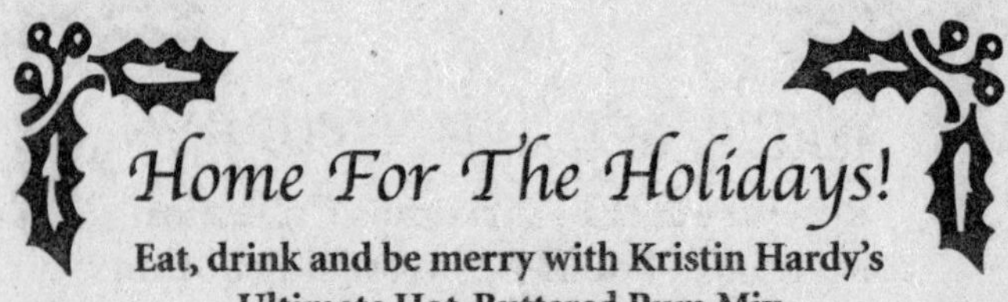

Home For The Holidays!

Eat, drink and be merry with Kristin Hardy's Ultimate Hot-Buttered Rum Mix

Treats make the holiday bright

One of my favorite holiday treats is hot-buttered rum. Not just any old hot-buttered rum, though. This is the ultimate, as revered by J. J. Cooper in *Under the Mistletoe* (Special Edition, December 2005). You'll be seeing J.J. again, so keep an eye out for him.

Hot Buttered Rum Mix

1 lb butter
1 lb white sugar
1 lb brown sugar
dash salt
1 qt light cream
1 tsp vanilla

add:

Hot Buttered Rum

1 tbsp Hot-Buttered Rum Mix
1 shot dark rum (Myers is good)
Hot water

Cream butter, sugar and salt until emulsified. You want it light and fluffy, as if making a cake, so don't rush. Combine cream and vanilla. Add about a half cup at a time and let blend in thoroughly before adding more. It should have the consistency of buttercream at the end. Makes about four cups.

To make hot-buttered rum, add the hot-buttered rum mix and a shot of dark rum (I like Myers) to a mug. Fill the rest of the way with hot water. Delicious.

Note:
This recipe makes enough to share. I put it in glass jars with a pretty label on the front with directions and a ribbon around the lid. It's an instant holiday gift, and one that almost everyone will love. For more recipes, go to www.kristinhardy.com.

SSERECIPEKRISTIN

Home For The Holidays!

While there are many variations of this recipe, here is Tina Leonard's favorite!

GOURMET REINDEER POOP

Mix 1/2 cup butter, 2 cups granulated sugar, 1/2 cup milk and 2 tsp cocoa together in a large saucepan.
Bring to a boil, stirring constantly; boil for 1 minute.
Remove from heat and stir in 1/2 cup peanut butter, 3 cups oatmeal (not instant) and 1/2 cup chopped nuts (optional).
Drop by teaspoon full (larger or smaller as desired) onto wax paper and let harden.
They will set in about 30-60 minutes.
These will keep for several days without refrigerating, up to 2 weeks refrigerated and 2-3 months frozen.
Pack into resealable sandwich bags and attach the following note to each bag.

I woke up with such a scare when I heard Santa call…
"Now dash away, dash away, dash away all!"
I ran to the lawn and in the snowy white drifts,
those nasty reindeer had left "little gifts."
I got an old shovel and started to scoop,
neat little piles of "Reindeer Poop!"
But to throw them away seemed such a waste,
so I saved them, thinking you might like a taste!
As I finished my task, which took quite a while,
Old Santa passed by and he sheepishly smiled.
And I heard him exclaim as he was in the sky…
"Well, they're not potty trained, but at least they can fly!"

HARRECIPETINA

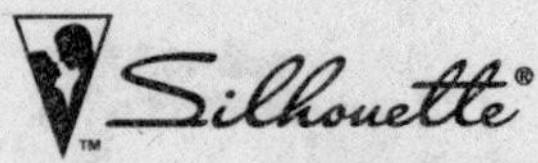

SPECIAL EDITION®

COMING NEXT MONTH

#1723 THE SHEIK AND THE VIRGIN SECRETARY—Susan Mallery
Desert Rogues
Learning of her fiancé's infidelities the day before her wedding, Kiley Hendrick wanted revenge—and becoming mistress to her rich, powerful boss seemed like the perfect plan. At first, Prince Rafiq was amused by his secretary's overtures. But when he uncovered Kiley's secret innocence, the game was *over*—the sheik had to have this virgin beauty for his very own!

#1724 PAST IMPERFECT—Crystal Green
Most Likely To...
To Saunders U. dropout Rachel James, Professor Gilbert had always been a beacon of hope. So when he called asking for help, she was there. Rachel enlisted reporter Ian Beck to dispel the strange allegations about the professor's past. But falling for Ian—well, Rachel should have known better. Would he betray her for an easy headline?

#1725 UNDER THE MISTLETOE—Kristin Hardy
Holiday Hearts
No-nonsense businesswoman Hadley Stone had a job to do—modernize the Hotel Mount Eisenhower and increase profits. But hotel manager Gabe Trask stood in her way, jealously guarding the Victorian landmark's legacy. Would the beautiful Vermont Christmas—and meetings under the mistletoe—soften the adversaries' hearts a little?

#1726 HER SPECIAL CHARM—Marie Ferrarella
The Cameo
New York detective James Munro knew the cameo he'd found on the street was no ordinary dime-store trinket. Little did he know his find would unleash a legend—for when the cameo's rightful owner, Constance Beaulieu, responded to his newspaper ad and claimed this special charm, it was a meeting that would change their lives forever....

#1727 DIARY OF A DOMESTIC GODDESS—Elizabeth Harbison
With new editor-in-chief Cal Paganos shaking things up at 125-year-old *Home Life* magazine, managing editor Kit Macy worried her sewing and etiquette columns were too quaint to make the cut. So the soccer mom tried a more sophisticated style to save her job...and soon she and Cal were making more than a magazine together!

#1728 ACCIDENTAL HERO—Loralee Lillibridge
After cowboy Bo Ramsey left her to join the rodeo, words like *commitment* and *happily-ever-after* were just a lot of hot air to Abby Houston. To overcome her heartbreak, Abby turned to running the therapeutic riding program on her father's ranch. "Forgive and forget" became her new motto—until the day Bo rode back into town....